Charles E. Benham

Colchester Worthies

a biographical index of Colchester

Charles E. Benham

Colchester Worthies
a biographical index of Colchester

ISBN/EAN: 9783337368623

Printed in Europe, USA, Canada, Australia, Japan

Cover: Foto ©Andreas Hilbeck / pixelio.de

More available books at **www.hansebooks.com**

COLCHESTER WORTHIES.

A

˙BIOGRAPHICAL INDEX

OF

COLCHESTER.

BY

CHARLES E. BENHAM.

LONDON:

SIMPKIN, MARSHALL, HAMILTON, KENT & CO., LIMITED.

COLCHESTER:

T. FORSTER, HIGH STREET.

PRINTED BY

BENHAM AND CO.,

at the

COLCHESTER PRINTING WORKS.

The following pages do not profess to contain by any means a complete list of the distinguished names connected with the town of Colchester. No one, however, having as far as I know endeavoured to compile any sort of Index of Colchester Worthies, I have felt justified in gathering together, as well as I could, some particulars of a few more or less noted Colchester characters, and shall be grateful for any suggestions, corrections or additions from my readers, in view of a possible further edition at some future time.

C.E.B.

45, *Wellesley Road,*
Colchester.

COLCHESTER WORTHIES.

AIRY, SIR GEORGE BIDDELL. Born at Alnwick, July 27, 1801. His younger days were spent at Colchester, where he was educated at the Royal Grammar School and also at a school in Sir Isaac's Walk. He lived in George Street, in a house now divided into two, Nos. 10 and 11, and on one of the upstair windows of the front of the house his autograph was until recent years visible, he having scratched it on the glass with a diamond. He went to Trinity College, Cambridge, and took his M.A. degree in 1826. He developed special taste for Astronomy and prosecuted that study with much vigour and success, being appointed Astronomer Royal in 1835, a post which he resigned in 1881, receiving a pension of £1,100 a year. He was knighted in 1872. Died Jan. 2, 1892.

ALFORD, EDWARD. Member for Colchester in 1627. He took part in the debate on the " Petition of Rights "—boldly exclaiming—" Let us give that to the King which the law gives him, and no more."

ALLEN, ROSE, Martyr, burned at Colchester on the afternoon of Aug. 2, 1557.

APLETON, SIR HENRY. A royalist officer in the siege, taken prisoner by Fairfax.

ARRAGON, CATHERINE OF. This queen visited Colchester in 1516, on her way to Walsingham, where she was going on a pilgrimage to the famous image of the Virgin there. She was conducted by the bailiffs, aldermen, and a number of burgesses, from Lexden to the town. She stayed the night at St. John's Abbey. The townspeople made her a voluntary present of £40, and on her departure the bailiffs, aldermen, and others again attended her as far as Milend.

AUDELEY, SIR HENRY. Lord of the Manor of Berechurch. His estates were sequestrated by by Parliament.

AUDELEY, HENRY. Inherited the family estates, but his life was a melancholy one, his vices proving his ruin, for he died a prisoner in the Fleet in 1714, having long been parted from his wife, a daughter of Viscount Strangford. A friend going to see him found that he was dead and about to receive a prisoner's burial. He stopped the funeral and communicated with the widow, who allowed £80 for a funeral and the body was buried at Berechurch.

AUDELEY, SIR THOMAS, Lord Chancellor of England. The Monks of St. John's Abbey, in hopes of appeasing his rapacity, alienated to him part of the domains of the Abbey, viz. :—Berechurch Hall and the Manor of Gosbecks, in Stanway. He was born of obscure parents at Earls Colne in 1488, was brought up to the law and made Town Clerk of Colchester in 1516, and a Free Burgess in 1526. He was Autumn Reader of the Inner Temple and became Speaker of the House of Commons in the Parliament that began Nov. 3, 1529. He made himself a great favorite of Henry VIII, and in 1530 was constituted King's Attorney for the Duchy of Lancaster. He advanced to higher and higher dignities and succeeded Sir Thomas More as Lord Keeper of the Great Seal. In 1532 he was knighted and the next year made Lord Chancellor. He was very zealous in the dissolution of the Monasteries and obtained from the King the sites of St. Botolph's Priory, Crouched Friers and other valuable possessions in Colchester. In 1538 he was made Baron Audeley and installed Knight of the Garter. He died in 1544, aged 56, and was buried at Walden.

BALL, J. A priest, who was one of the rebels in Wat Tyler's insurrection and became one of the chief incendiaries. He made Colchester a place of refuge because he had followers in that town. It is said that the charge brought against him, though nominally for high treason was really for heresy, and that he was the first known Wycliffist martyr. Executed at St. Alban's, July 15, 1381. To encourage the rebels Ball used the lines:

> "When Adam dolve and Eve span,
> Who was then the gentleman?"

BARKSTEAD, COL. A Parliamentarian officer who fought bravely at the siege in 1648. One of the Forts was called "Barkstead's Fort," on the Maldon Road. He was M.P. for Colchester in the reign of Charles I.

BARNARDISTON, ARTHUR. Recorder of Colchester in the time of Oliver Cromwell. He died in 1655.

BARNARDISTON, J. A royalist officer in the siege. He tried to make terms with Fairfax, but it was then too late, and the Parliamentarians would not entertain his conditions. It is curious that the Barnardiston family (who have been seated in Suffolk from the time of the conquest) are traditionally connected with the origin of the appellation Roundhead, which it is said was, from the beauty of his person, first bestowed on Samuel Barnardiston, a distinguished partizan of the parliament in the reign of Charles II.

BARNES, JOHN STUCK. For many years Clerk of the Peace for the Borough. Born in St. Leonard's Parish, 1806. Though a zealous nonconformist, he placed a stained glass window in St. Leonard's Church, to the memory of his father. He died Feb., 1887.

BARRINGTON, SIR THOMAS. M.P. for Colchester in the reign of Charles I.

BASTWICK, DR. JOHN. He lived in Red House, Eld Lane, near the Baptist Meeting House. He wrote some books against Popery, which proved disagreeable to the Court and brought him into considerable trouble. He was fined £1000 and costs. His book was burned and he was excommunicated and imprisoned for 2 years. Born at Writtle, near Chelmsford, 1593.

BATCHELOR, HENRY. Yeoman, of Colchester. He bequeathed £60 a year to three preachers in Colchester. The will bears date 1646-7.

BECHE, JOHN. The last Abbot of St. John's. He would not subscribe to the King's supremacy and was hanged for high treason at Colchester,

Dec. 1, 1539. He was invited by the bailiffs of the town to a feast, and in the midst of the proceedings his death warrant was disclosed to him.

BENNOLD, THOMAS. A tallow chandler, burned on the morning of Aug. 2, 1557, outside the Town Walls.

BERNARD, WALTER. A tenant of the Severalls, and Alderman and Sheriff of London.

BESTNEY, BARKER. Lived at Monkwick. His estates were sequestrated by Parliament.

BIGOD, ROGER. Earl of Norfolk. Earl Marshal of England. Constable of the Castle, 1258.

BONGEOR, WILLIAM. A glazier, of St. Nicholas Parish, burned, outside the Town Walls, on the morning of Aug. 2, 1557.

BUCKLER, GEORGE. An architect, who took great interest in the archæology of Essex. The ablest exponent of the theory of the Roman origin of the Castle. Wrote "Colchester Castle a Roman Building," "Twenty-Two Churches of Essex," &c. Died in London, Sept. 2, 1886, aged 74. Interred in Nunhead Cemetery. His father was a clever topographical artist.

BULL, JOHN and RICHARD FARNHAM. Two Colchester Weavers, who about 1640 declared themselves to be the two great prophets mentioned by the prophet Zachariah, and the Two Witnesses spoken of in Rev. xi. 3. They claimed that they had power to shut up heaven so that it should not rain, and to smite the earth with plagues, and said that they should not die out of Jerusalem and that after three days and

B

a half their dead bodies would rise, and Richard Farnham would be King on David's throne and John Bull priest in Aaron's seat, and that they would reign for ever. They both died in the plague, and the few converts whom they had made declared that the two prophets had gone in vessels of bulrushes to convert the ten tribes, and would return and rule England with a rod of iron.

BRADENHAM, LIONEL DE. Endeavoured to enclose and appropriate the Colne Fishery in the reign of Richard I. His attempt was resisted by Robert de Herle, Lord Admiral, in revenge for which he attempted to reduce the town to ashes. These exploits, however, soon brought about his ruin, and he was compelled to screen his forfeited life under a pardon.

BREE, CHARLES ROBERT (M.D., Edin.) For 22 years Physician to the Essex and Colchester Hospital. Resided at Colchester during that time, 1859-81, after which he left the town for Long Melford, where he died, Oct. 17, 1886, aged 75. He was the son of Mr. John Bree, of Keswick, and he married the daughter of Sir Augustus Henniker, Bart. He was the author of several valuable works on Natural History, and published treatises against the Darwinian Theory, to which he was strongly opposed. He was part editor of the *Naturalist*, and for many years a Fellow of the Linnean and Zoological Societies. He was J.P. for Essex and Suffolk.

BROWN, JOHN. A Colchester stone mason, who carried on business for about 25 years on East Hill. He was born at Braintree in 1780. From boyhood he evinced great interest in geology and when he had saved enough money he purchased a house and farm at Stanway, where for the remainder of his life he devoted himself to his favorite subject. When over 70 years of age he tried to learn French. He was a frequent contributor to scientific journals. He discovered some huge fossil bones at Lexden, which he presented to the British Museum. At his death he left £300 to the Geological Society of London, £100 to the Geologists' Association, and all his books, collections and cabinets, together with £50, to Professor (now Sir Richard) Owen (one of his executors) on the understanding that the specimens were to be deposited in museums, at the discretion of the Professor. Died Nov. 28, 1859. Buried in Stanway Churchyard.

BROWN, ROBERT. Member of Parliament for Colchester in the reign of Queen Mary, who with 36 other members voluntarily left the house on the passing of an act repealing acts against the supremacy of Rome.

BUXTON, ROBERT. An apothecary, who founded the trade of candied eryngo roots, a kind of sweetmeat of a medicinal character prepared from the root of the sea holly (Eryngium maritinum.) It was considered a stimulant and restorative, and was for some time a renowned Colchester product. He died 1655 and was buried in St. Nicholas Church.

CAMPES, ABBOT ADAM DE. Lived in the reign of Edward I. He cunningly asked to see the Charter of the Lepers Hospital at Colchester and then flung it in the fire, taking away the common seal of the Hospital and enforcing an oath of obedience to him. Redress was however subsequently obtained from Parliament.

CAMPION, COL. SIR WILLIAM. A royalist officer, killed in the siege 1648. A rumour of his death reaching his wife, she bravely approached the camp of Fairfax in person and obtained leave to send a letter into the town to ascertain the truth. There is a monument to him in St. Peter's Church.

CAPEL, LORD ARTHUR. A nobleman, son of Sir Henry Capel, Knight. He represented the county of Hertford in the Parliament of 1640. In the civil war he became such a zealous royalist that the House of Commons confiscated his estates. He was one of the noblest of the defenders in the siege of 1648, and on the surrender of the Town he was imprisoned in the Tower, from whence he escaped, but was re-captured and beheaded March 9, 1649. His literary remains were published in 1654, with the title of " Daily Observations or Meditations." They are full of deep pious fervour, and he was also the author of some beautiful verses published in Lloyd's Memoirs of Remarkable Sufferers.

CARR, SAMUEL. A grocer, born in Boxford, 1732, settled in Colchester, where he died in 1809. He was the first to introduce Sunday Schools and to encourage the culture of potatoes in this part of the county. A portrait of his wife, by Gainsborough, was, a few years ago, I believe, exhibited in the Gainsborough Exhibition in London.

CARR, SAMUEL PUPPLETT. Son of Samuel Carr, born 1750, died 1823. He was one of the first to introduce the manufacture of gas into Colchester. He erected gas works in the rear of his premises, No. 11, High Street, Colchester, to supply his own premises. He also laid down the first tramway for trucks in the town. He owned all the wharfage from the Hythe Bridge to the Bonding Warehouse on the south side of the river.

CATCHPOOL, RICHARD D. A native of Colchester, though the greater part of his life was spent at Reading. He always took a lively interest in his native town, in which he was a property owner. and offered £1,000 towards a New Town Hall, in Jubilee year, 1887, but the inhabitants rejected the scheme. He left generous bequests to Colchester, conditionally on the money being devoted to a Public Library and Recreation Ground. Died Nov. 7, 1890, aged 68.

CHAMBERLAYNE, NICHOLAS. A Martyr, burned at Colchester, June 1557.

CHIVELYNG, WILLIAM. A tailor, burned in Colchester for heresy, by order of King Henry VI.

CHURCHE, ROGER. A prior of the convent of Crouched Friers.

CLAUDIUS. The Roman Emperor. Founded Colchester (Camulodunum) about 50 A.D. to serve as a monument of the victory there, which had made him master of the southern part of the island.

COCKE, WILLIAM, was threatened with suspension for not yielding to wear the surplice at his church of St. Giles. Buried in St. Giles's Church, 1619.

COEL, KING. The mythical "Old King Cole," traditionally associated with Colchester, from a fancied derivation of the word—Coel's castra, or camp.

COLCHESTER, ELIAS FITZ JOHN DE. First M.P. for Colchester in the reigns of Edward I and II.

COLCHESTER, HUBERT DE. M.P. for Colchester in the reign of Edward I.

COLCHESTER, JOHN OF. Rector of Tendring and Prior of the Convent of Crouched Friers. He founded a chantry in St. Helen's Chapel in 1321, and one in St. Mary's Church, the funds of which were afterwards devoted to the founding of a Free School.

COLCHESTER, LORD (Charles Abbot). Born, 1757. Son of Rev. John Abbot, D.D., Rector of All Saints, Colchester. His mother (née Sarah Farr,) was married secondly to Jeremy Bentham. Charles Abbot was, in 1801, appointed Chief Secretary to the Lord Lieutenant of Ireland, and keeper of the Privy Seal in Ireland. In 1882 he became Speaker of the House of Commons, and filled the Chair till 1817, when he was elevated to the peerage, with the title, Baron Colchester. Died May 7, 1829.

COOK, COL. A Volunteer in the Royalist Forces at the siege in 1648.

COOK, REV. MOSES, of Sible Hedingham. He left £800 for the augmentation of the living of St. James.

COMPTON, HENRY, Bishop of London. Youngest son of the Earl of Northampton. Born 1632. He was very zealous against popery. He performed the ceremony of crowning William and Mary in Westminster Abbey. It was a saying of his that " the Church is for the living, the Churchyard for the dead," the meaning of which is more obvious in his own funeral, which, by his own wish, was humbly carried out in Fulham Churchyard, 1713. He was the author of several learned theological works, and made a generous bequest of valuable books to the Colchester Corporation, but with intolerable meanness they would not be at the expense of the carriage, and his heir was consequently obliged to sell them, and they were thus lost to the town.

COMPTON, SIR WILLIAM. A Royalist officer in the siege of 1648.

COWPER, EARL WILLIAM. Lord Chancellor of England, born in Hertfordshire. He rose rapidly at the bar, and was made Recorder of Colchester. In 1705 he was made Keeper of the Great Seal. He was made a peer in 1706, an earl in 1718, and died Oct. 10, 1723. Buried at Hertingfordbury.

COX, CAPT. An old, experienced cavalry officer on the Parliamentarian side, killed at the siege on the 13th of June, 1648.

COX, JOSEPH. Died 24 June, 1689, leaving £5 per annum to the poor of St. Mary's, to be distributed every Christmas day.

CREFFEILD, LADY. Wife of Sir Ralph Creffeild. She made a bequest to the poor of Trinity Parish.

CREFFEILD, SIR RALPH. Alderman and three times Mayor of Colchester. He was knighted by Queen Anne on presenting her with an address of thanks from the Corporation on the conclusion of the peace of Utrecht. He married Rachel, daughter of

George Tayspill. Died June 22, 1732, aged 79. Buried in St. Nicholas Church.

CREFFEILD, RALPH, Jun., J.P., died 1723. aged 36. Second son of Sir Ralph Creffeild. His daughter Hannah married G. Wegg. (q.v.) Buried in St. James's Church.

CROMWELL, THOMAS, Earl of Essex, son of a blacksmith, born at Putney, 1490. He entered into the service of Cardinal Wolsey, who obtained him a seat in the House of Commons. When the Cardinal fell he became a servant of the King, who conferred upon him knighthood and other honours. In 1536 he received the title of Lord Cromwell. On the dissolution of the monasteries he received the grant of many manors, and among them those of Milend and Greenstead. In 1539 he was created Earl of Essex, soon after which his fortune rapidly declined. His ruin was hastened by the marriage which he projected between Henry and Anne of Cleves, and he was sent to the Tower and finally beheaded, July 28, 1540.

CUNOBELIN. The Cymbeline of Shakespeare, whose Royal town was Colchester, previous to the appearance of Claudius.

DAMARIN, WILLIAM. Principal coachman to the Emperor of Russia for upwards of 5 years and for many years coachman of the Royal Mail from London to Colchester. Died 1844. Buried in St. Mary's Churchyard.

DANIELL, JEREMIAH. A resident in the Town, who died 1696, aged 61, and bequeathed an annual gift of coals to the poor of several parishes. Buried in St. Peter's Church.

DARCY, MARY, LADY. Lived in Trinity parish opposite the West end of the Church. She died in 1644, and bequeathed to the town some Almshouses in Eld Lane. She was daughter of Sir Thos. Kitson, of Hengrave, and wife of Viscount Colchester, Earl Rivers.

DARCY, SIR THOMAS, Kt. Was granted a 21 years' lease of the site of St. John's Abbey, Aug. 29, 1544, on the dissolution of the monasteries.

DARCY, THOMAS, BARON. Created Viscount Colchester, July 5, 1621, with a grant of £8 out of the fee farm of the town. He was advanced to the title of Earl Rivers, Nov., 1626. Died, Feb. 21, 1639.

DAVIDS, REV. THOMAS WILLIAM. Congregational Minister at Lion Walk Chapel for 34 years. Born at Swansea, Sept. 11, 1816. He was an eminent historian of Essex Nonconformity, and his works evince considerable research and careful study. Died in London, April 11, 1884. Buried in Colchester Cemetery.

DE CLERK, W. Returned to Parliament as Burgess, 34 Edw. I. and 4 Edw. II.

DE FOE, DANIEL. The celebrated author of Robinson Crusoe and the "Shortest Way with Dissenters." Born, 1663, in Cripplegate. He held the Severall's or King's Wood Heath on a 99 years' lease, from August, 1722. His tenancy also included Brinckley Farm and Tubbeswick, the rent being £120 and a fine of £500. Among his other works, which were of a very varied character, he wrote an interesting account of a tour through the Eastern Counties, which contains a full account of the Siege of Colchester and many other particulars about the town, evincing the observant faculties which characterised the man.

DICKMAN, ROBERT. A Vicar of St. Peter's, who records in the parish register an extraordinary earthquake on the 8th of September, 1692.

DISTER, AGNES, made a bequest to the poor of the parish of St. Peter, in which church she was buried, in 1553.

DUGARD, WILLIAM, of Sidney College, Cambridge. A most industrious and successful Master of the Grammar School, an appointment which he received in 1637. He did much for the good of the school, but received such abuse and ill usage in return, that he had to resign in 1642-3.

DYER, SIR LODOWICK. A royalist officer, taken prisoner in the Siege, 1648.

EDWARDS, JOHN. A Colchester clergyman, chosen Lecturer to the Corporation in 1700, at a salary of £50 per annum.

ELIANOR (or Alianor), JOHN. M.P. for Colchester in the reign of Edward III.

ELIANORE, JOSEPH. M.P. for Colchester. Founded a chantry in St. Mary's Church, in Feb., 1348. He was several times bailiff of the town. At the reformation the advowson was utilised for founding a Free School.

ELIZABETH, QUEEN, visited Colchester, Sept. 1 and 2, 1579.

ERNULPH } A Monk, founder of St. Botolph's
EYNULPH } Priory, and its first Prior. He introduced into England the Order of Regular Canons of St. Augustine.

EUDO, DAPIFER (Steward Eudo). Son of Hubert de Rie, who was a servant and favorite of William the Conqueror, to whom he was of great service in assuming the English throne. The reward of his services came to his son Eudo, who, besides receiving large possessions was made Steward of the Household. Inheriting in full measure the tact and skill of his father he succeeded in securing the throne to William II. The Town of Colchester, realising that he would therefore be a favoured subject of that monarch, petitioned for him as their Governor, so that they might be under his protection and free from the hardships which they had had to endure in the past. This was granted the Town, and he resided there in High Street. Opposite his residence he built the Moot Hall, pulled down in 1843. He was Lord of the Manors of Greenstead and Berechurch. The great work of his life was the founding of the monastery of St. John's Abbey. He chose the site of this building in a remarkable manner. A little wooden church stood there, at which strange miracles were said to be performed. There, too, on dark nights, heavenly lights were often seen and voices when no-one was within, and on one occasion, on the feast of St. John, a man, who was kept there in fetters, by command of the king, was miraculously freed from his chains, which flew off of their own accord. Pondering over his project, therefore, he determined that this must be the site of the Abbey and St. John its patron saint, and the work of building was accordingly begun in 1096, and the next year, after Easter, Eudo himself reverently laid the first stone. Amongst other manors in his possession he devoted the revenues of Berechurch to the Abbey. With the first Monks there he had considerable trouble, on account of their discontent and ill behaviour, and finally he committed the whole monastery into the hands of Stephen, Abbot of York. With the King's consent, and in his presence, he bequeathed to the monastery the Manor of Bright-lingsea, £100 in money, his gold ring with a topaz, a cup, with cover adorned with plates of gold, together with his horse and mule. He also founded the Leper's Hospital, in the Parish of St. Mary Magdalen. He died at the Castle of Preaux, in Normandy, and at his own desire was buried in his beloved monastery, at Colchester, Feb. 28, 1120. His wife was Rohaise, daughter of Richard, son of Gilbert, Earl of Eu. They had one daughter, Margaret, who married William de Mandeville.

EVELYN, JOHN, the well known writer, visited Colchester in 1656, and described the town as "wretchedly demolished by the late siege, especially the suburbs, which were all burnt, but were then repairing." He testifies to the spot alleged then to be the death place of Lucas and Lisle, which he says was "bare of green for a large space, all the rest of it abounding with herbage." Of the baize and says trade he says, Colchester "is the only place in England where these stuffs are made unsophisticated." (That is, genuine).

EWER, COLONEL. An officer under Fairfax in the siege, 1648. He was sent at the conclusion of the siege to the King's Head Inn, to fetch Lucas, Lisle, and Gascoigne, and to prepare them for their fate. He told Sir Charles Lucas, with a slighting gesture, that the General desired to speak with him at the Council of War, and also with Sir George Lisle, Sir Bernard Gascoigne, and Col. Farre. The latter, however, had made his escape. The others went with him and were told that they were condemned to be shot to death.

EWRING, HELEN. A martyr, burned outside the town Walls, on the morning of Aug. 2, 1557.

FACILIS, MARCUS FAVONIUS. A Roman centurion, whose finely sculptured effigy and monumental inscription, found at Colchester, is by far the most valuable of all the Roman cemetery memorials found in the neighbourhood. The relic is in the possession of Mr. George Joslin of Colchester.

FAIRFAX, THOMAS, LORD. General of the Parliamentarian forces at the siege in 1648. He was the eldest son of Ferdinando, Lord Fairfax, and was born at Denton, Yorks., 1611. He married the daughter of Lord Vere. He was a literary man, and fond of antiquarian researches, which latter predilection, no doubt contributed to his evident desire at the siege to avoid unnecessary destructive combat, for he made many offers for peace, on conditions, which, considering the strength of his position, were by no means ungenerous. His terms were not, however, accepted, and at last, when the town was forced to a surrender, and was evidently completely in his power, he, in turn, declined the proffered terms of the besieged. He succeeded to the family estate and honours a year previous to the siege. In the Civil War generally he played an important part, and contributed to the victory of Naseby, after which he subdued the whole of the West of England. He died at his seat in 1671. He was the author of several poems, and a volume of memoirs published in 1699.

FARNHAM, RICHARD. (See John Bull.)

FARR, COLONEL. A royalist officer in the siege 1648. He escaped from the Town just previous to its surrender.

FISON, JAMES. A musician and composer, who died at East Bay, about 1849, in the 99th year of his age. He received a pension for his musical acquirements and services.

FITZWALTER, ROBERT, BARON. Lord of the manor of Lexden. He founded the monastery of Grey Friars, and in 1325 entered there as a religious votary. He died there the following year.

FOLKS, ELIZABETH. A martyr burned outside the Town Walls on the morning of Aug. 2, 1557.

FRANCKHAM, ROBERT. Bequeathed a gift to the poor of the parish of St. Nicholas.

FRAUNCEY, THOMAS. Founded a chantry in St. Nicholas Church, by will dated 1416. Among the stipulations was one that a lamp was to be kept continually burning in the Church by day and night before the cross, and a wax light before the image of St. Nicholas at mass time.

FYNCHE, JOHN. M.P. for Colchester in the reign of Edward III.

FYNCHE, RALPH. A brewer, who lived at the bottom of Balkerne Hill. He endowed four almshouses in St. Nicholas parish.

GASCOIGNE (or Guasconi) SIR BERNARD. A native of Florence. A royalist officer in the siege. He tried to make a sally from the Town with Lucas and Lisle, and all the volunteers and horse of the garrison, on July 15, 1648. They crossed the river at Middle Mill and tried to get to Nayland, but their guides misled them, and roused the enemy. The guides and the pioneers then fled, and they were all obliged to retreat. Sir Bernard was condemned to death with Lucas and Lisle, but at the last was reprieved as not being an Englishman.

GEORGE, CHRISTIANA. The last martyr burned at Colchester, May 26, 1558.

GILBERD, GYLBERD, GILBERT, HIEROME (or Jerome.) Father of the celebrated Dr. Gilberd (see below.) He lived at Clare, in Suffolk. Was Recorder of Colchester, of which town he was made a free burgess in 1553. Died May 23, 1583.

GILBERD, THOMAS. Grandfather of Dr. Gilberd, born at Hintlesham, and made a free burgess of Colchester in 1428.

GILBERD, DR. WILLIAM. Son of Hierome Gilberd. He was born in 1540, and studied at Oxford and Cambridge. He afterwards travelled into foreign countries, where he took his degree, and returned famous for his learning. He was made an M.R.C.P., London, and Chief Physician to Queen Elizabeth, who valued him very highly, and allowed him an annual sum to encourage him in his studies. He was also Chief Physician to James I. In 1600 he published his famous book, " De Magnete," the first work ever written on Electricity. It evinces immense sagacity and genius, and in it the word "electric" was first given to the world. In this work, too, appears the important discovery of the variation of the magnet. He also wrote a book, "De Mundo nostro sublunari Philosophia nova," which was published at Amsterdam after his death. He invented two instruments for finding the altitude without the help of sun, moon, or stars. He died Nov. 30, 1603, and was buried in the chancel of Trinity Church, where there is a monument to his memory. He had four brothers—Ambrose, William, a Proctor in Arches; Hierome, and George.

GILBERT, GEORGE. Made a bequest to the poor of All Saints parish.

GILBERT, MRS. (neé Ann Taylor). Daughter of Rev. Isaac Taylor (q.v.) Lived in Stockwell Street 1796-1811. Married Rev. J. Gilbert, 1814. Her first literary venture was before her marriage, when, in conjunction with her sister Jane, she wrote the well-known "Hymns for Infant Minds," full of a terse simplicity which soon rendered them successful. Encouraged by this success, she followed it up with many more poems, some of which (such as "My Mother" and "Twinkle, twinkle little Star,") have become "familiar in our minds as household words." Her "Rhymes for the Nursery" were spoken of in high terms by Sir Walter Scott. She was also the author of prose writings less well known. Died at Nottingham, 1866.

GILSON, DANIEL. First Minister at the Presbyterian Chapel, St. Helen's Lane. Died 172⅞.

GLISSON, DR. FRANCIS. A learned physician, born at Rampisham, 1596, who for some time lived in

St. Mary's Parish. He removed to London, and died there, 1677. He wrote five medical treatises, and was President of the College of Physicians. He was the discoverer of Glisson's capsule, a membrane investing the portal vein, hepatic artery, and hepatic duct. During the siege Dr. Glisson was sent by the council of war at the siege to propose arbitration to Fairfax, but the appeal was made too late.

GORING, LORD, Earl of Norwich. A prominent royalist in the siege. On June 4, 1648, news came into the Town, that he, with Lord Capel and 2000 of the loyal party, who had been in arms in Kent, were coming by Greenwich and Stratford to Colchester. Sir Charles Lucas, Sir George Lisle, Col. Cook, and others at once resolved to join them as a band of volunteers to fight for the King. He reached Colchester on the 10th of June. The people there sympathised chiefly with the Parliamentarians, and were with difficulty prevailed upon to admit the royalists, but at last, on certain conditions they submitted, and the troops entered and made the place their headquarters, causing drums to beat for volunteers. Lord Goring encamped at first in the suburbs, and on the 12th he came into the town and brought in Sir William Masham and other prisoners. He acted with intrepidity and with some lack of prudence, refusing the offer of the engineers to entrench his camp, though afterwards, when a battle was at hand and there was no time to do it, he would probably have been glad of the protection. His sanguine boldness was further evinced in his refusal to exchange prisoners with the enemy on account of his expectation that re-inforcements would come to his aid. On the 20th

June, Fairfax again offered terms, which Lord Goring contemptuously and laughingly declined. More than once Fairfax sent a protest that poisoned bullets had been used by Lord Goring's direction, an accusation which Lord Goring indignantly repudiated. Further offers of treaty from Fairfax he also declined, and on the 12th of Aug. the people crowded round his quarters, clamouring for surrender, and they repeated their demonstrations of dissatisfaction every evening. At last surrender became inevitable, and Goring was among the prisoners of the enemy.

GRAY, CHARLES. M.P. for Colchester in five parliaments, in the reigns of George II. and III. He purchased the Castle of Isaac Leming Rebow, and was diligent in preserving this valued antiquarian relic. Died, Dec. 12, 1782, aged 86. Buried at All Saints. He constructed the domed tower and the Library at the Castle, and founded in the latter, in 1750, the Castle Society Book Club; among whose members was Morant. He also purchased a great part of the Castle Lands.

GRAY, MYLES. A Colchester bell founder of the 17th Century.

GREAT, SAMUEL. An apprentice to Robert Buxton (q.v.,) after whose death he carried on the eryngo root trade. He died in 1706, aged 80, and was buried in St. Nicholas' Church.

GRIFFIN, REV. LEWIS, M.A. A Colchester divine and Master of the Grammar School. He occupied a benefice (Greenstead) during the plague. He was author of several poems—one entitled—" The

Doctrine of an Ass," containing the following couplet :—

> " Devils' pretences always was divine,
> A Knave may have an Angel—for a sign."

Died at Colchester about 1670.

GRIMSTON, SIR HARBOTTLE. Born at Bradfield, 1594. He bought the site of Crouched Friars in 1637, and made it his place of residence. The house was battered down and burned in the siege in 1648. His father (Harbottle Grimston) was made Baron in 1612, and free burgess of Colchester in 1625. The son was brought up to the law and made M.P., 1639, when he spoke vehemently against the grievances of the town. After his house had been destroyed in the siege he travelled abroad. He was afterwards made Speaker in the " Healing Parliament," April 15, 1660, and continued to represent Colchester till his death in 1683. In Nov., 1660, he was made Master of the Rolls. He published the Reports of Sir George Croke, whose daughter he married. He gave £20 for the relief of the poor in the plague in 1655-6. He was elected M.P. for the County as well as the Borough, and for part of his parliamentary career he chose to stand for the County, Sir Robt. Quarles taking his place as Member for the Borough.

GULL, SIR WILLIAM WITHEY. This eminent physician was born at Colchester and baptised at St. Leonard's. He was the son of a mariner, and soon after his birth his parents removed to Thorpe-le-Soken, where he was brought up at the village school. He chose a schoolmaster's career, and assisted for a time in teaching at a Mr. Seaman's school in Colchester. He then went to teach at a school at

Lewes, and rapidly developed great scientific tastes, which gained him a post at Guy's Hospital, in connexion with cataloguing the museum. This led him to devote his attention to medicine, and having taken his degree, he soon rose to distinction. He attended the Prince of Wales, with Sir William Jenner, throughout a dangerous attack of typhoid fever, and his successful services were rewarded with a baronetcy. He married in 1848 the daughter of Col. J. Dacre Lacy. Died Jan. 29, 1890.

HALE, —. A descendant of Sir Matthew Hale, and an inhabitant of Colchester, who in 1832, constructed a steamboat which was exhibited in September of that year on Virginia Water, before the King and Queen and various members of the Royal Family, who took great interest in the invention.

HAMO, DAPIFER. One of the earliest property owners in Colchester.

HAMMOND, COL. EDWARD. A royalist officer made prisoner in the siege in 1648.

HAMMOND, J. A tanner, burnt at Colchester, April 28, 1556.

HARRIS, W. A martyr, burned at Colchester, May 26, 1558.

HARRISON, RALPH. Alderman of Colchester at the time of the siege in 1648. Buried in St. Botolph's.

HARSNET, DR. SAMUEL. Archbishop of York. Born in 1561, in St. Botolph Street. He was son of William Harsnet, a baker, and was probably educated in the Town. In 1576 he went to King's College,

Cambridge. Thence he went to Pembroke Hall, of which he was elected a Fellow in 1583, and the next year he took the degree of M.A. In 1586 he was chosen Master of the Free School at Colchester, a post he held little more than a year and a half. He became Vicar of Chigwell, which he resigned in 1605. In 1598 he was made a Prebendary of St. Paul's Cathedral and in 1602 Archdeacon of Essex. In 1604 he became Rector of Shenfield and subsequently Rector of St. Margarets, New Fish Street, London. In 1605 he succeeded Bishop Andrews as Master of Pembroke Hall and in the same year, and in 1614, he served the office of vice-chancellor. In 1606 he became Vicar of Hutton and afterwards he was Rector of Stisted. In 1609 he became Bishop of Chichester and in 1619 was translated to Norwich. He was accused by the Puritans of Arminianism, and in 1624 the Commons found fault with him for several misdemeanours. In 1628 he became Archbishop of York, and died at Morton-on-the-Marsh, May, 1631. He was buried at Chigwell, where he had founded a Free School, and amongst other bequests he left £10 to the poor of St. Botolph, and all his library to the town for the use of the Clergy. His own writings include a Sermon condemning Absolute Predestination, and an attack on the "fraudulent practices" of certain individuals whom he accused of the "deceitful trade" of "casting out devils." Morant describes his works as being written with great strength of reason and elegantly "considering the times" (which, by the way, were "the spacious days of Queen Elizabeth.") The condition on which he bequeathed his Library to the Town, was that a decent place should be provided for it. It was placed in the Dutch Say Hall over the Red Row. This was in 1631. In 1654-5 all the books were mortgaged to the Chamberlain for £50. In 1664 it was resolved that the Grammar School Master should have charge of the books and be responsible for them. They were afterwards removed to the Castle, where they have been ever since, and have recently been repaired and catalogued at great expense. Unfortunately some are lost. They include a fine Antwerp Bible, and Hesychius with Isaac Casaubon's M.S. notes, and many other valuable works.

HARVEY, DANIEL WHITTLE. Member of Parliament for Colchester, returned in 1818, 1820, 1830, 1831, and 1832. He was born at Kelvedon, and commenced his career at Colchester as an articled clerk to Mr. Peter Daniell, solicitor, at Head Gate. He early developed considerable talent for public speaking. He became a somewhat ardent radical, and was so zealous at public meetings in furtherance of radical opinions, that he was induced to contest the Borough in 1812, but was defeated by the Conservative candidates. His determination and perseverance, however, urged him not to abandon his attempts, which were afterwards more successful, and he was several times returned at the head of the poll. He was subsequently appointed by the Corporation of London, Chief Commissioner of the City Police. He held this office simultaneously with his seat in Parliament, until the passing of the New Police Act, when he was no longer eligible for the House of Commons, and consequently in 1834, he retired from the representation of Colchester, and retained his official appointment till his death, which was in about 1864.

HARVEY, JOHN BAWTREE. Three times Mayor of Colchester. He was born at Ipswich, 1809, and there commenced his career. Came to Colchester in 1837, and was for some years engaged in Liberal journalism in the town. He took a special interest in gas lighting, and was Chairman of the Colchester Gas Co. Died at Colchester, Aug. 10, 1890.

HASTINGS, HENRY, Lord Loughborough. A royalist officer made prisoner in the siege, 1648.

HAWES, REV. THOMAS. Rector of St. Leonard's ; gave some books to the Town in 1635.

HAY, JAMES, Earl of Carlisle. Was given the reversion of the Castle by Charles I., Aug. 5, 1629.

HENEAGE, SIR THOMAS, Kt. Held King's Wood Heath, or the Severalls, Milend, under lease in accordance with the express desire of Queen Elizabeth.

HELENA, EMPRESS. The Mother of Constantine the Great. Mythically associated with the History of Colchester, probably because of her supposed relationship to the legendary King Coel (q.v.)

HERRICK, JOSEPH. Pastor of the Presbyterian Chapel in St. Helen's Lane, 1812-4. In 1814, Mr. Herrick and the congregation removed to the present Stockwell Chapel, while seceders from the old methodist body took the old meeting house and elected a minister.

HEWITT, REV. CHARLES. A Greenstead clergyman of whom E. P. Strutt in his " Colchester Celebrities of the Olden Times " tells a story, that on one occasion he went to sleep in the pulpit, and when the congregation had all gone out, the clerk said, " They are all out, sir." " Oh, are they ? " said the parson, half awaking, " fill them up again, my brave boys ! "

HICKERINGILL, REV. EDMUND. For 46 years Rector of All Saints. Died in 1708, and was buried in all Saints Church. A long complimentary epitaph in Latin was inscribed on his tomb, a portion of which, was, it is said, afterwards effaced by order of Bishop Crompton. He was a staunch opponent of the Civilians. He was cited before Sir Robert Wiseman to answer certain irregularities in the performance of his clerical duties. He entered Westminster Hall, June 8, 1681, to answer this charge, with his hat on, and was commanded by Sir Robert Wiseman to be uncovered. Mr. Hickeringill replied in Greek to this and all Sir Robert's remarks. He afterwards repeated in English all he had said in Greek. He was again commanded by Sir Robert to be uncovered, and as he refused, an old fellow, a kind of sumner, was ordered to snatch it from his head ; but Mr. Hickeringill snatched it back and clapped it on his head again, and held it there all the time he was in court, throwing down a protest against the proceedings, which was read out.

HOLBEYE, MARGARET. In the reign of Queen Elizabeth she was indicted for exercising " the art of fascination as well of men as of animals, and for having caused Elizabeth Pickas, by her diabolical practices, to waste away." She was imprisoned for a year, and put in the pillory once a quarter, on market days.

HONEYFOLD, DR. GABRIEL. A Master of the Lepers' Hospital and Vicar of Ardleigh. At the beginning of the Civil Wars, his house was rifled by the mob, and every atom of his belongings taken from him ; the register being also destroyed.

HONYWOOD, SIR THOMAS. An officer under Fairfax in the siege in 1648.

HUMPHREY, PRINCE. Duke of Gloucester and Protector of England. Constable of Colchester Castle, 1404. He is supposed to have been murdered in 1447.

HUNWICK, JOHN. An alderman of Colchester, who left, in 1593, £300 for the poor, lame, and impotent, in Colchester.

HURNARD, JAMES. A well-known member of the Society of Friends, who resided at Hill House, Lexden, and was before that a brewer on East Hill. He was an ardent Liberal, and was rewarded for his zeal in that cause by being made an Alderman in the Town Council. He was a man of literary tastes, and from time to time indulged in poetical efforts. His principal venture in this way was a volume in verse, entitled—"The Setting Sun," dealing somewhat incisively with local affairs. Died, Feb. 26, 1881, aged 73. He married, somewhat late in life, and left one son.

HURST, EDMUND. A resident in St. James's parish ; burned at Stratford, June, 1556.

INGRAM, THOMAS. Made a bequest to the poor of St. Peter's parish.

IRETON, COLONEL HENRY, son of German Ireton. He was born at Attenton, Notts., 1610. He married a daughter of Oliver Cromwell. He fought under Fairfax at the siege in 1648, and was at the Council of War at which Lucas and Lisle were condemned to die. He died in Ireland of a fever, exclaiming in his last moments, " Blood, blood ! " He died Nov. 26, 1651. His body was brought to England, and buried in Westminster Abbey; but at the Restoration it was taken up, suspended on a gallows, and then thrown into a pit with those of Cromwell and Bradshaw. He is described as a dark, treacherous, and hypocritical character.

JARVIS, DR. JOHN. Rector of Greenstead in 1644. Depositions were taken against him, when it was affirmed on oath, amongst other graver charges, " that he had often said this Parliament are a company of factious fellows, who aim at nothing but their own ends, and that he was not able to deliver anything in his sermons, more than what he read out of his book, pointing with his fingers for the most part to every line." The living was sequestrated, August, 1645.

JENKINS. REV. HENRY, of Stanway. A zealous exponent of the theory of the Roman origin of the Castle. He held that it was the actual Temple of Claudius. Died, 1874. His arguments were inconclusive, wild and inaccurate, and found few adherents (see Buckler.)

JENNENS, JOHN. A claimant of the enormous estates of William Jennens, of Acton Place. The important chancery suit, in connection with these estates, formed the original of " Jarndyce v. Jarndyce" in Dickens's *Bleak House*. John Jennens died at Colchester, 1769, and was buried in St. Peter's Churchyard. The tombstone bears the text, Jer. ix, 6, " Through deceit they refuse to know me."

JOBSON, SIR FRANCIS. A resident at Monkwick, from whom John Lucas bought the site of St. John's Abbey. He bought the monastery of the Grey Friars after the dissolution of the monasteries. Died at Monkwick, 1573, and was buried in St. Giles's Church.

JOHNSON, ABRAHAM. M.P. for Colchester in the first Parliament of Richard Cromwell, 1659.

JOYNE, SIMON. A sawyer, burned at Colchester, April 28, 1556.

JOHNSON, JOHN. A martyr, burned at Colchester on the afternoon of Aug. 2, 1557.

JUDDE, LADY MARY, of Latton. A native of Colchester, who left £100 for the benefit of the poor of the town.

KENDALL, JOHN. A wealthy member of the Society of Friends, who was largely instrumental in founding, in 1791, Almshouses for the widows whose husbands had died in Winsley's Almshouses.

KNEVETT, THOMAS. Suspended for preaching at Milend without a license, having been admitted to the rectory on the presentation of Sir Thomas Lucas in 1584.

LADELL, EDWARD. A famous Colchester Artist, son of a coachbuilder on East Hill. His Still Life has a world wide reputation, and in his lifetime his studio was always represented at the Royal Academy. Died Nov. 9, 1886, aged 65.

LANVALLEI, WILLIAM DE. Lord of the Manor of Stanway, and founder of the Convent of Crouched Friars about 1244. He was also constable of Colchester Castle.

LAWRENCE, JOHN. A martyr, burned at Colchester, March, 29, 1555.

LAWRENCE, NATHANIEL, Jun. Son of Nathaniel Lawrence, who was several times Mayor. He was lame for seven years, and suddenly recovered the use of his legs. Died 1750-1, aged 90.

LAYTON, SIR WILLIAM. A royalist officer taken prisoner in the siege in 1648.

LEOFLEDA. A wealthy lady whose name appears in the Domesday Survey, as the richest of the 276 King's burgesses. She owned three houses, 25 acres, and a mill, probably on the site of the present East Mills.

LEWIS, Son of Philip II. of France, made himself for a short time master of the Castle and Town, and all the Eastern parts of England, 1218.

LISLE, COLONEL SIR GEORGE. One of the chief defenders in the siege in 1648. He was condemned to death by the Parliamentarian Council of War, and was shot outside the Castle immediately after the execution of Sir Charles Lucas. He knelt by the body of his gallant comrade in arms and kissed him, then rising, uttered his well known protest—" Oh, how many of your lives who are now present here, have I saved in hot blood, and must now myself be most barbarously murdered in cold ! " Bestowing a small gift on his executioners, he bade them approach nearer, so that they might do their work more completely. "I'll warrant ye, sir, we'll hit you," exclaimed one of them. "Friend," said Sir George, calmly, "I have been nearer when you have missed me." Buried with Sir C. Lucas in St. Giles's Church.

LOVELESSE, FRANCIS. Master of the Ordnance in the siege in 1648. He was made prisoner by Fairfax.

LUCAS, CHARLES, BARON. Son and heir of Sir Thomas Lucas, of Lexden, Knight. He was Lord of the Manor of Lexden, and lived there at the Tenterhouse. He married a daughter of the Earl of Scarsdale.

LUCAS, SIR CHARLES. Younger brother of Sir John Lucas. He was brought up for a military career, in the Low Countries, under the Prince of Orange, and became one of the best commanders of Horse that King Charles I. had. He fought for that monarch in several places, and notably in the Siege of Colchester, at the end of which he was shot by command of Fairfax, outside the Castle, Aug. 28, 1648 (vide Sir G. Lisle.) He was a stern and staunch man throughout his life, and his last words were—"See, I am ready for you. Now, rebels, shoot!" Pierced by four bullets, he fell dead. He died childless.

LUCAS, SIR JOHN. An officer of King Charles; eldest son and heir of Sir Thomas Lucas, jun. He lived at St. John's. On Aug. 22, 1642, as he was preparing to go with a detachment of cavalry to the King in the North, he was barbarously used by some of the inhabitants, who plundered his house, desecrated the ashes of his ancestors in St. Giles's Church, and took him prisoner to London. Being released, he fought for Charles I. at Lestwithiel and Newbury, and in other battles, in consideration of which he was made a Baron in 1644-5, with the title of Lord Lucas of Shenfield. Died, 1671, and was buried in St. Giles's Church.

LUCAS, JOHN. Third son of Sir Thomas Lucas; was Town Clerk of Colchester, and Master of the requests to Edward VI. He bought the site of St. John's Abbey of Sir Francis Jobson. He was also Lord of the Manor of Milend, and died, 1556.

LUCAS, LADY ANNE. Wife of Lord John Lucas, Baron of Shenfield. Buried in St. Giles's Church. Died, Aug. 22, 1660.

LUCAS, SIR THOMAS. Sheriff of Essex in 1568, and Recorder of Colchester in 1575. He generously entertained the Earl of Leicester on his visit to the town, Dec. 6, 1585. His estates at Lexden were sequestrated by the House of Commons, because he would not accede to certain Parliamentary measures.

LUCAS, SIR THOMAS, Jun. Son of the above. Sheriff of Essex in 1617. He purchased for his son, Thomas, the manorial estates at Lexden and placed him there.

MACE, JOHN. An apothecary, burned at Colchester, April 28, 1556.

MARGARET, QUEEN, of Anjou, was granted Colchester Castle by Henry VI., in 1447.

MARSDEN, CANON JOHN HOWARD. Resided many years at Grey Friars, East Hill. Born, 1803. He was a distinguished scholar, and attained high honours at Cambridge, where he won the First Bell's Scholarship in 1823, and the Seatonian prize for English verse. He held the appointments of Select Preacher to the University of Cambridge in 1834, 1837, and 1847, was Hulsean Lecturer in 1843 and 1844, and Disney Professor of Archæology, 1851 to 1865. In 1840 he was presented to the Rectory of Great Oakley. He was the author of several works, including his two volumes of Hulsean Lectures, the Life of Sir Simon D'Ewes, archæological lectures, and a collection of poems, entitled Fasciculus. He was a celebrated authority on archæological and numismatic subjects. Died, Jan. 24, 1891, aged 88.

MARSH, REV. WILLIAM, D.D. For 15 years Vicar of St. Peter's. He was born, July 1775, being the third son of Col. Sir Charles Marsh, K.C.B. His mother, "Dame Catherine Marsh," who died at Colchester in 1824, married at the early age of 16. She was the daughter of Mrs. Case, a friend of the poet Pope, and a lady of cultured intellect. Dr. Marsh came to Colchester from Brighton in 1816. He married Maria Tilson in 1806. He took a deep interest in Missionary work to the Jews. He was a powerful speaker and a most popular man in the town. When he left Colchester in 1829, a noble presentation of plate and the sum of £1000 was presented to him by the inhabitants of Colchester. Died August, 1864, having passed 64 years in the ministry. He was buried at Beddington. His life and letters were published in 1867 by his daughter, who was also the author of the "Memorials of Capt. Hedley Vicars."

MASHAM, SIR WILLIAM. An officer under Fairfax, taken prisoner by the Royalists at the commencement of the siege. He sent a message to Fairfax, entreating him to treat for peace. The Parliamentarians offered a prisoner named Ashburnham in exchange, but the proposal was rejected. Sir Wm. Masham was M.P. for the town in the reign of Charles I.

MAULYVER, SIR RICHARD. A royalist officer in the siege of 1648. He was taken prisoner by the Parliamentarians, escaped, and was re-captured.

MORANT, REV. PHILIP. The celebrated historian of Colchester. Born in Jersey in 1700, and educated at Abingdon School, whence he removed to Pembroke College, Oxford, where he took the degree of M.A. in 1724. He held several livings in Essex, the principal one of which was that of St. Mary's, Colchester. He was an indefatigable antiquarian, and his famous compilation—The History of Essex, including The History of Colchester, also published in a separate volume, has preserved an immense wealth of local history. He was also one of the compilers of the Biographica Britannica, and was appointed by the House of Lords to publish a copy of the Rolls of Parliament, which work, at his death, devolved upon his son-in-law, Mr. Astle. He died in London, in 1770.

MOTT, ALDERMAN. A burgess who was disenfranchised for disdemeanours in 1694. One of these misdemeanours consisted in his having made a person a free burgess without consent of the Common Council.

MOUNT,⎫ ALICE & WILLIAM. Two martyrs
MUNT, ⎭ burned at Colchester on the afternoon of Aug. 2, 1557, after being imprisoned awhile in the Castle.

MUSCHAMP, MAJOR. A royalist, killed in the siege, 19th June, 1648.

NAGGS, WILLIAM. Made a bequest to the Charity Schools at Colchester. Died July 30, 1758, aged 80. Buried in St. Peter's Churchyard (south side).

NEEDHAM, COL. A Parliamentarian officer who commanded the Tower Guards in the siege, and was killed in the action of June 13, 1648.

NETTLES, STEPHEN. A Rector of Lexden in the 17th century, whose property was sequestrated by Parliament.

NEWCASTLE, MARGARET Duchess of (née Margaret Lucas). Daughter of Sir Charles Lucas. She was born at St. John's, Colchester. She was afforded a complete education, and early in life exhibited taste for literature. She was the second wife of William Cavendish, Earl, Marquis, and Duke of Newcastle, to whom she was married in 1645. Two years before this she visited the Court of Charles I., then at Oxford, was appointed one of the maids of honour to the queen and accompanied her majesty to France. She published ten folio volumes of letters, plays, poems, philosophical discourses, orations, and the life of her husband the duke. Her life was distinguished by pious and charitable works. Died in London, 1673, and was buried in Westminster Abbey.

NELSON, LUKE. An eccentric cobbler and antiquarian who lived in St. Mary's parish. His portrait appears in Strutt's Celebrities, at the Colchester Museum. Died Feb. 22, 1805, aged 69. Buried in St. Mary's Churchyard.

NEWCOMEN, THOMAS. Rector of Holy Trinity in the middle of the 17th Century, and Chaplain to Sir John Lucas. He was sequestrated for his loyalty to the King in 1642, but obtained redress on the restoration.

NICHOLS, R. A weaver, burned at Colchester, April 28, 1556.

NORTHYE, GEORGE, of Clare Hall. Chaplain to the Colchester Corporation, 1580. He was suspended for a year by the Bishop of London. Died, 1593. Buried at St. James's.

ORILEY, SIR HUGH. A royalist officer in the siege of 1648, taken prisoner by the Parliamentarians.

PARNEL, JAMES. A quaker, who came to Colchester when 18 years old, in 1655, and preached with great zeal and success. His tenets drew upon him the charge of heresy, and he was imprisoned in the Castle, and suffered great hardships and indignities, being confined in a chamber in the wall some 12 feet from the ground, with a ladder 6 feet long as his only means of descent for food. In attempting to get out from this miserable cell, he fell and was nearly killed. He suffered continued and increasing hardships, till at last death ended his sufferings.

PARR, DR. SAMUEL. A master of the Colchester Grammar School, 1776-8, during part of which time he held the cures of the parishes of Holy Trinity and St. Leonard's (the Hythe). He was a man of unrivalled classical erudition, and a very voluminous writer. He was the author of the epitaph to Dr. Johnson in St. Paul's Cathedral. His wife used to say of him, that he was "born in a whirlwind and bred a tyrant." The ardour of his temper, with his fulness of knowledge, made him a fluent speaker, and he often preached extempore at Colchester, his custom being to avoid any preparation of his subject, which he selected from any passage that struck him in the lessons, epistle, gospel, or psalms of the day. Born at Harrow, Jan. 15, 1746-7. Died at Hatton, March 6, 1825.

PEPPER, ELIZABETH, of St. James's Colchester. A martyr, burned at Stratford, June, 1556.

PIGG, OLIVER. Vicar of St. Peter's and Rector of All Saints, from 1569 to 1570, in which year he removed to Abberton. He was committed on the charge of putting the question in the Baptismal Service, " Dost thou believe ? " not to the child, but to the parents. He finally conformed to the law and was discharged.

PRICE, SERJEANT, L.L.D. Recorder of Colchester in 1722, or rather Deputy of Earl Cowper, who was Lord High Chancellor, and who did not reside in the Borough. Dr. Price lived at Tymperleys, in Trinity Street, the former residence of Dr. Gilberd (q.v.)

PURCAS, WILLIAM, of Bocking. A martyr, burned at Colchester, outside the Town Walls, on the morning of Aug. 2, 1557.

QUARLES, SIR ROBT., Kt. M.P. for Colchester in the reign of Charles I. Grandfather of the poet, Francis Quarles.

QUINCEY, SAHER DE, Earl of Winchester. He brought an army of foreigners into the country, and besieged Colchester Castle in 1215, but hearing that the Barons at London were hastening to its relief, he withdrew to Bury St. Edmunds. However, he or another party soon afterwards made themselves masters of Colchester, and plundered it, as they had done Ipswich and other places. But after a few days' siege, the King (John) re-took it, coming in person to Colchester with what forces he could muster.

RATCLIFF, JOHN. Lord of the Manor of Lexden, 1440-1494. In 1485 he received the title of Lord Fitzwalter, and unhappily engaged in a conspiracy to set Perkin Warbeck on the throne. He was convicted of high treason, and obliged to forfeit all his estates, though they were afterwards restored to his son, the Earl of Sussex. He was beheaded at Calais.

RAWLINS, LIEUT.-COL. GEORGE. A royalist officer taken prisoner in the siege in 1648.

RAWSTORN, SAMUEL. Lived at Lexden, and died, 1719-20. He married Sarah, daughter of Thomas Papillon, of Acris, in Kent.

RAYNHAM, JOHN. Mayor of Colchester in 1705. He admitted 96 foreigners to the freedom of the Borough on his own authority, and swore them in privately without the Town Clerk, for which reason they lost their freedom.

REBOW, SIR ISAAC. Son of John Rebow. M.P. for Colchester in the reigns of William and Mary, Anne, and George I. He lived at Head Gate. He was made High Steward and Recorder in 1693, and also served as Mayor. Died, 1726. He purchased Colchester Castle of John Wheely, 1704.

REBOW, ISAAC LEMING. M.P. for Colchester in the reigns of George II. and III. Son of Sir Isaac Rebow. Died, 1735.

REBOW, ISAAC MARTIN. Son of Isaac Leming Rebow. Recorder and M.P. for Colchester. Died, 1781. Buried in St. Mary's Church.

REBOW, JOHN. A Colchester merchant. Married Sarah, daughter of Francis Tayspill. Died, 1699, aged 71, and was buried in St. Mary's Church, where there is a monument to his memory, erected by Sir Isaac Rebow.

REYNOLDS, SAMUEL. M.P. for Colchester in the reign of Charles II. He lived in St. James's parish. Died, 1694.

RUSH, SAMUEL, of London, a vinegar merchant, gave, in 1711, £100 for purchasing a building for the Charity Schools of Colchester, and, in 1741, his widow bequeathed £50 to the Schools.

ROUND, CHARLES GRAY. M.P. for North Essex. Inherited the Castle, 1834, and presented the "Chapel" to the Town for a Museum and one of the mural chambers for a Record Room. Died, 1867.

ROUND, REV. JAMES THOMAS, B.D. Born in St. James's parish, July 14, 1798. Second son of Mr. Charles Round. He became classical tutor at Balliol College, Oxford, and subsequently rector of St. Nicholas and St. Runwald. He was appointed Rural Dean in 1840, and an Hon. Prebendary of St. Paul's in 1843. He resigned the living of St. Nicholas in 1846, and, in 1851, his college presented him to the Rectory of All Saints, Colchester, and, in 1858, he re-built the Rectory house of that parish. The Chancel and part of the nave of St. John's Church was built by a fund raised to his memory after his death, which occurred Aug. 27, 1860. He edited a collection of the prose works of Bishop Ken, and was the author of a commentary on the four Evangelists.

ROUND, JOHN. Recorder of Colchester. Third son of William Round, J.P., of Birch Hall. Born, June 20, 1736. Died, Nov. 9, 1813. Buried at St. Martin's.

ROUND, GEORGE. Son of George Round, J.P., of Lexden House. Born, 22nd March, 1803. Died, 1857. He was appointed High Sheriff of Essex in 1845. Married Margaret, daughter of Major-Gen. W. Borthwick, R.A., of Dedham.

ROUND, CHARLES, J.P., of Birch Hall, Colchester Castle, the Holly Trees, &c. Born, July 31, 1770. Died, April 18, 1834. Son of James Round, of Birch Hall.

ROUND, CHARLES GRAY, J.P. and D.L., Essex. Son of Charles Round (q.v.) Born, Jan. 28, 1797. He was Recorder of Colchester, owner of Colchester Castle, and Lord of the Manors of Great and Little Birch, and Chairman of the Essex Quarter Sessions for 27 years. Contested Oxford University against Mr. Gladstone in 1847. Died, Dec., 1867. Married Jemima Sarah, daughter of Major G. Brock, of Colchester.

SAMBROOK, LT.-COL. A royalist officer killed in the siege, July 5, 1648.

SAVAGE, JOHN, Viscount Colchester. Grandson of the Earl of Rivers (see Darcy,) and succeeded to his title, Feb., 1639.

SAVAGE,, RICHARD. The last Viscount Colchester. Died, Aug. 18, 1712.

SAVAGE, THOMAS. Son of John Savage. Succeeded to the title. Died, Sept., 1694.

SAYER, GEORGE. An alderman, and one of the bailiffs of the town. He was possessed of several estates in the country. He gave 4 almshouses to the town (in Balkerne Lane) in 1570. They had no endowment, and have long been taken down. He was Grandson of John Sayer (q.v.) who, though a younger son, obtained possession of his father's estate in consequence of the flight of his elder brother to Holland, owing to religious persecution in the reign of Henry VIII. George Sayer died in 1577, and was buried with his ancestors in St. Peter's Church, where a remarkable monument to his memory may be seen. The family of Sayer or Sears is found located in the vicinity of Colchester in the early part of the 13th Century, and possessed then of considerable estates. Other members of the family were Sir George Sayers, died 1650, and Richard Sayer, buried in St. Peter's, 1610.

SAYER, JOHN. A Colchester Alderman, died 1509. Buried in St. Peter's Church.

SHAWE, SIR JOHN. A prominent royalist during Cromwell's Government. Lived in the parish of All Saints. He was brought up to the law, and at the Restoration was made Recorder of Colchester, a post which he resigned Nov. 12, 1677. He was three times M.P. for the town, and died 1690, aged 73. Buried in Trinity Church.

SHIPMAN, SIR ABRAHAM. A royalist officer, made prisoner in the siege, 1648.

SILVERSIDE, AGNES. A martyr, burned at Colchester, outside the Town Walls, on the morning of Aug. 2, 1557.

SIRIC ⎞ A Priest whose wooden church was
SIGERIC ⎠ on the site on which Eudo afterwards founded St. John's Abbey.

SKINNER, DR. THOMAS. Physician to General Monk. Lived in All Saints parish. He was the author of " Motus Compositi," " Life of General Monk," and other works. Buried in St. Mary's Church, Aug. 8, 1679.

SMITH, SAMUEL. A Colchester tailor, who was so frightened by a practical joke in the shape of a person in a white sheet, that his mental faculties were deranged, and he became a well-known local eccentric, who went about the streets making speeches. On one occasion, for inciting riot at Dedham, he was condemned to the stocks, and pretending more madness than he was really victim to, he got the constable to show him how to put his feet in the stocks, and then promptly locked the unhappy officer in and escaped to Colchester. Finally, a delusion that he had committed a robbery, led him to commit suicide by hanging. The date of his birth and death is not known, but he was a contemporary of E. P. Strutt, who gives a short account of him in his note book of Colchester Celebrities.

SPURGEON, REV. CHARLES HADDON. The famous Baptist Pastor of the Metropolitan Tabernacle. He was born at Kelvedon, June 19, 1834, his parents being strict Congregationalists. His father, John Spurgeon, was in business, and settled in Colchester about 1840. His mother was a Colchester woman (youngest sister of Mr. C. P. Jervis, of Colchester.) The Rev. C. H. Spurgeon, who early left the sect to which his parents belonged, and joined the Baptists, became a preacher whose name is of world wide reputation. He frequently visited his native County and Colchester. After a lingering illness, he died at Mentone, Jan. 31, 1892.

SPENCE, JOHN. A weaver, burned at Colchester, April 28, 1556.

STANHOPE, SIR JOHN. Treasurer of the Chamber to Queen Elizabeth, who granted him Colchester Castle.

ST. CLARE, HUBERT DE. One of the earliest Constables of Colchester Castle. He fought for King Henry II. at the Siege of Bridgenorth, and thrust himself between the King and one of the enemy, so that he saved the King and received his own death wound. The King gave Hubert's daughter in marriage to William de Lanvallei, with her father's inheritance.

STEPHENS, JOHN. Counsellor at Law, J.P., and of the Quorum. Lived at Crouched Friars. Died, 1620.

STEPHENS, JOHN, Jun. Counsellor at Law. Lived at Crouched Friars, and died 1626.

STOCKTON, OWEN. Born at Chichester, May, 1630. At the age of 16, he went to Christ's College, Cambridge, and was a pupil of the celebrated Henry More. He was introduced to Charles I., who said,

G

" Here is a little scholar indeed, God bless him ! "
He chose to become an itinerant preacher, and rose to
such fame, that the Mayor of Colchester, Thomas
Laurence, and the Corporation, invited him to be
their Chaplain, a post which he accepted ; and
preached also on Sunday mornings at St. James's,
without fee. He removed from Colchester after this,
but returned and took out a license in 1672, to be a
Presbyterian and Independent Teacher in St. Martin's
Lane, Colchester. He was the author of many
M.SS. and publications. Died, Sept. 10, 1680.

STORY, GEOFFREY. A bold and turbulent
Abbot of St. John's, imprisoned for high treason in
the 6th year of Henry IV.'s reign. He was carried
from his chamber to the Moot Hall in a chair, being
ill at the time, and there imprisoned for five weeks,
and was afterwards taken to Nottingham Castle.

STOW, HENRY, of Lexden. Famous for his
auriculas, said to have been the finest in the Kingdom,
if not in all Europe. Some of them had 133 blossoms
on a single stem. He also grew magnificent tulips.

STRUTT, SIR DENNARD. A royalist officer
taken prisoner in the siege of 1648.

STRUTT, BENJAMIN. Chamberlain of Colchester
in the early part of the 18th Century. He was
familiarly known as "Ben Strutt," and like his son,
E. P. Strutt (q.v.,) was fond of composing verses and
making caricature sketches of local celebrities.

STRUTT, E. P. Son of Benjamin Strutt (q.v.)
A Colchester worthy who had the gift of making
clever caricatures of his local contemporaries in the
18th Century. A small note book containing these

was given by Strutt to the late Mr. J. E. Tabor, and is now in the Colchester Museum. It contains portraits (among many others) of Capt. Crane (who fought at Bunker's Hill), Petticoat John (bell toller at St. Giles's), Luke Nelson (q.v.,) Doctor Mann, John Dunthorne (a local artist and a friend of Constable), Samuel Smith (q.v.,) John Hall (an old soldier), and Lieut. John Andrews (who was interviewed at Lexden Heath by the Duke of York on the occasion of an inspection of troops. "How old are you, Andrews? said the Duke, "Ninety years," said Andrews, "and have been in the service 70 years. His Royal Highness asked how long he had worn his suit of Regimentals. "About 40 years," replied Andrews. The Duke felt the cloth, and remarked that such was not made now-a-days. "No, nor such men neither," said the veteran.") E. P. Strutt died in Winsley's almshouses.

SUMMERSUM, THOMAS WILSHIRE. A centenarian, born at the Hythe, Nov. 19, 1791 ; died at Brightlingsea, Feb. 13, 1892. His grandfather, Thomas Wilshire, was Mayor of Colchester in 1765, and was the first to wear the Mayor's Chain of Office (presented by Mr. Leonard Ellington, an eminent bay factor of London, and a member of the Society of Friends). As a boy, Summersum journeyed on a barge to London from the Hythe, and while on the Thames, witnessed the arrival of the remains of Nelson, brought to London for interment in St. Paul's Cathedral. He left Colchester at the age of 24, and passed the remainder of his life at Brightlingsea, where, in November, 1891, there was an enthusiastic demonstration and banquet in honour of the completion of his hundredth year, when the old man delivered a stirring speech and sang the National Anthem.

SYMSON, REV. BARNABAS, M.A. Rector of St. James's for 25 years. Died, 1741-2.

TABOR, JAMES ASHWELL, J.P. A member of an old Colchester family. Born Dec. 2, 1789. He took great interest in local philanthropic work, and was one of the originators of the museum. It must also be mentioned, though the fact perhaps hardly redounds to his credit, that he was instrumental in effecting the removal of the Moot Hall and Middle Row. He established the Colchester Ragged Schools. Wrote "Memoir of Charles Burgess Harwood," "Lecture on Rivers," "Improvement of the Colne Navigation," "History of Lion Walk Independent Church," "Nonconformist Protest," and "What is Truth." Died at his residence in Crouch Street, Nov. 1, 1881.

TAYLOR, ANN (see Mrs. Gilbert).

TAYLOR, REV. ISAAC. An independent minister who came to Colchester in 1795. He was the author of poems and prose works, the best known of the latter being on " Self-Cultivation." He was father of the well known Jane and Ann Taylor, the latter of whom became Mrs. Gilbert (q.v.) He lived in a house now divided into two, just below St. Martin's Church, in West Stockwell Street. Died Dec. 12, 1829.

TAYLOR, ISAAC. Son of Rev. Isaac Taylor. Wrote "Natural History of Enthusiasm," and other minor works. He lived in Stockwell Street, Colchester, 1796 to 1810. Died June, 28, 1865.

TAYLOR, JANE. Sister of Ann Taylor (Mrs. Gilbert), and daughter of Rev. Isaac Taylor. Lived in Stockwell Street, Colchester, 1796-1811. Wrote

"Essays in Rhyme," and other volumes of poems. Died 1824.

THURSTON, JOHN.   Died a prisoner for religion in the Castle, in 1557.

TUKE, COL. SAMUEL.   "A man of honour and integrity."   Towards the close of the siege, in 1648, he was sent out, with J. Barnardiston, to Fairfax, to ask him to agree to the terms he had previously offered, but it was too late.   Fairfax, feeling that he then had the power in his own hands, declined all terms.

TWINING, REV. THOMAS.   A Rector of St. Mary-at-the-Walls in the 18th Century.   He published in 1789 a translation of Aristotle's Poetics, and in 1790 a History of the Pharisees.   A record of his career will be found in a work published by Mr. John Murray, under the title of " A Country Clergyman of the 18th Century."   Born Jan., 1734. Died, August, 1804.

ULWINE.   A Colcestrian, and the only bearer of the venerable title of *monitor*, or crier, recorded in Domesday.

VERE, JOHN DE.   Earl of Oxford and Constable of the Tower of London.   The Fishery at Colchester was bestowed upon him by Henry VI.   He was made Constable of the Castle, 1496.

VILLIERS, GEORGE, Duke of Buckingham. He married Fairfax's only daughter.   There is a tradition that he applied to Charles II. to have the tablet erased, which is in St. Giles's Church, to the memory of Lucas and Lisle.   The matter was referred to Lord Lucas, who said he would willingly erase it if they would put in its place that Lucas and Lisle were barbarously murdered for their loyalty to Charles I., and that his son Charles II. ordered the monument to be erased, whereupon the King ordered, that instead of being erased, the memorial should be cut even deeper than before, which was done, and accounts for the present depth of the lettering.

VITELS, CHRISTOPHER. A disciple of Henry Nicholas, of Delft, founder of a strange sect called "the family of love." Vitels established a branch of the sect in Colchester, in the reign of Queen Mary.

WALSINGHAM, SIR FRANCIS. This famous statesman, born in 1536, at Chislehurst, was Recorder of Colchester during the greater part of Elizabeth's reign. With all the services he rendered, and the distinctions he achieved, he died poor, April 6, 1590. He was buried in St. Paul's Cathedral.

WARREN, EDWARD. Ejected from the vicarage of St. Peter's about 1670, and practised physic in the town. Afterwards took out a license to be a Presbyterian teacher "at his own house, or John Rayner's, in Colchester." Author of several publications. Died, 1690.

WATERHOUSE, THOMAS. Ejected from the living of Ash, in Suffolk. He became Master of Colchester Grammar School (1643 to 1647) in succession to William Dugard.

WATSON, EDWARD. The first Master of the Grammar School. Appointed by the Corporation, 1585.

WATSON, J. YELLOLY, of Thorpe-le-Soken. Presented a valuable collection of Minerals to the

Museum, and wrote Sketches of Ancient Colchester and other valuable contributions to Local Archæology. Died, May 18, 1888, aged 70.

WATTS, SIR JOHN. A royalist officer made prisoner in the siege of 1648.

WEGG, GEORGE. A Colchester merchant tailor and Town Councillor. Lived in St. James's parish, in a house called Berryfield. He made a bequest to the poor of St. Nicholas parish, and was buried in that Churchyard, 1747, aged 82.

WENOCK, ⎫ JOHN. A bay-maker. Endowed
WINNOCK, ⎭ 6 almshouses in the parish of St. Giles's.

WHALLEY, COL. An officer under Fairfax in the siege in 1648.

WHEELER, JAMES. A churchwarden of St. Botolph's, who was twice excommunicated for refusing to rail in the communion table in 1635. He was imprisoned for three years, and his house broken up. Escaping from prison, the Mayor, Robert Buxton, had his family kept in custody, and his house ransacked in search of him. He died abroad, leaving his wife and children ruined.

WHEELY, JOHN, Jun. Purchased the Castle, May 9, 1683, for the purpose of destroying it, but finding the project too costly, abandoned it, and in 1704 sold the Castle to Sir Isaac Rebow.

WHITE, SIR THOS., Kt. Lord Mayor of London in 1553. Received the honour of Knighthood for preserving the peace of the city in Wyatt's rebellion. He made numerous liberal benefactions to various towns, including Colchester, in 1566.

WICKS, CAPT. A royalist officer taken prisoner in the siege, in 1648.

WINSLEY, ARTHUR, J.P. A Colchester Alderman, who founded and endowed 12 almshouses in St. Botolph's parish. He left £250 for a monument to be erected to him in St. James's Church, with his statue in marble, holding a book, on which are inscribed the words—" Go, and do thou likewise." Whether or not this injunction has been taken into consideration, the bequest has grown so that the number of houses is now increased to 18. Died, Jan. 30, 1726-7.

WIRE, WILLIAM. Son of John Wire, who died in Winsley's Almshouses, April, 1856. He was born, June 29, 1804. Died, April 1, 1857. He was a watchmaker in Colchester, and at the same time he dealt in all sorts of curiosities, being himself a zealous antiquarian. For 25 years there passed through his hands, the chief bulk of the coins, urns, and Roman remains found in the town, and as there was no local museum, these passed away to London, Oxford, and Cambridge, or to private collectors. William Wire kept a detailed account of all these relics, with drawings, in a valuable journal, which is now in the Colchester Museum. Mr. Wire was a good Anglo-saxon scholar, and a first-class numismatist. He corresponded with all antiquaries of note, and Mr. C. Roach Smith paid a graceful tribute to his memory in his " Retrospections," vol. II. Mr. Wire reprinted " Colchester's Teares," a rare tract written at the time of the siege, 1648. His shop was a place of resort for many leading men of science and archæology.

WIRE, DAVID. A native of Colchester, who became Lord Mayor of London, 1858-9. He commenced his career in London as an office boy with Mr. Daniel Whittle Harvey (q.v.), who seems to have skilfully gauged the lad's capacities, and induced him to leave Colchester. Died at Lewisham, 1860.

WOLTON, HENRY. A Colchester merchant, who held the office of Alderman, and was six times Mayor of the town. Died 1874, aged 71.

YETSWEIRT, NICASIUS. Secretary for the French tongue to Queen Elizabeth, who granted him the revenues belonging to the Lepers' Hospital, Colchester.

ERRATUM.

Page 41. The account of the Duchess of Newcastle is from the Biographia Britannica, though evidently "daughter" of Sir Charles Lucas is a misprint for *sister*. She was daughter of Sir Thomas Lucas.

'TYMPERLEYS' GILBERT'S HOUSE.

H

POST SCRIPT.

Several additions have come to hand too late for insertion in their proper place in the foregoing pages, and I have to thank Mr. Wilson Marriage (Mayor of Colchester), Mr. Henry Laver, F.S.A., Mr. James Round, M.P., and others for the following addenda:—

CHURCHILL, J. M. A Doctor resident in Colchester some 30 years ago, who was joint author of Stephenson & Churchill's Medical Botany—a standard work of reference.

CRISP, STEPHEN. Born at Colchester, 1628. He was converted to Quakerism by the preaching of James Parnell, the Quaker Martyr, in 1655, and was, for promulgating these opinions, imprisoned in the Moot Hall for a year. He travelled largely on the Continent, introducing his views in Holland and Germany. Married a German lady connected with the Princess Elizabeth of the Rhine. On the accession of Charles II., he was offered the post of Magistrate in Colchester. He died 1692, when on a visit to London, and was buried at Bunhill Fields. His collection of writings and a history of his life were published in 1694, by T. Sowle, at the Crooked Billet, in Holywell Lane, Shoreditch.

DUNTHORNE, J. "The Colchester Hogarth," as he was called. I am not able to give any detailed account of this worthy, but must refer my readers to Leslie's Life of Constable, in which I believe some interesting particulars about Dunthorne will be found. He lived in Colchester, at the end of the last century. Many of his water colour drawings still exist in Colchester. (His portrait is in the frontispiece).

GRAUNT, EDWARD, of Colchester. When attending a Meeting of the Society of Friends in Colchester, he was grievously injured by the Troopers sent to break up the Meeting, and died about a month afterwards, aged 70 years.

GRIFFITHS, DR. MOSES. Practised as a physician in Colchester, and published a Practical Treatise an Hectic Fevers and Pulmonary Consumption, written in Colchester in 1776 (newer edition, London, 1795). In this work is the original prescription for "Griffiths's Mixture," a · well known and useful recipe in the treatment of cases of debility. This formula has been adopted in the English, American, and Continental Pharmacopœias, under the name of *Mistura ferri composita*. It is still frequently prescribed. A likeness of him, by Dunthorne, is in Mr. F. Keeling's possession.

LAY, BENJAMIN. Born at Colchester, 1677. A Quaker, who travelled in many parts of the world, and obtained a private audience with King George II., in order to present to him an Essay on Milton. He was a man of peculiar physique, being but 4ft. 7in. in height, his head large in proportion to his body, hunch-backed, with a projecting chest, and very slender legs. His face was remarkable. He had a very active mind, and left England for Barbadoes, but was greatly shocked there at the horrors of the slave trade, and moved away to America after 13 years' residence, during which he never ceased to denounce slavery. He was intimately acquainted with Benjamin Franklin and other distinguished men. He wrote largely on Slavery, and may be said to be the first Anti-Slavery Advocate in America. He died at Abringdon, Pennsylvania, in 1759, aged 82 years, leaving a legacy to the Colchester Society of Friends, for enabling poor Quakers to emigrate to America, and to relieve distress in Colchester. He give directions for his body to be cremated, but his friends refused to carry this into effect. For a full account of this remarkable and eccentric man, see " Life of Benjamin Lay, by Robert Vaux," and other writers.

MACLEAN, ALLAN, M.D. Physician, Naturalist, and Horticulturist. Born at Sudbury, 1796. Died at Colchester, 1869. His knowledge of Natural History was very extensive, and he made important experiments in the propagation of fruit and vegetables. He raised the first white pelargonium, and his experiments with marrow fat peas enabled us to have that delicacy a month sooner than was before possible. His Early Red variety of rhubarb is also unsurpassed for its early fitness for table, as well as for its flavour. For many years he held the appointment of Physician to the Essex and Colchester Hospital.

NETTLES, STEPHEN (page 41). The " Essex Archæological Transactions " issued in March, 1892, state that this worthy was the author of a learned reply to the Jewish part of Selden's History of Tithes. He is mentioned in Walker's " Sufferings of the Clergy," as "a very smart and learned person." He was born 1584. Died 1654.

WEGG, G. To the account already given of this worthy on page 56, I should add that " Berryfields " is the present East Hill House, where there are portraits of George Wegg, his wife and niece, said to have been painted by Hudson, Sir Joshua Reynolds's master.

POSVERVNT HVNC TVMVLVM AMBROSIVS
& GVLIELMVS GILBERD IN MEMORIAM
PIETATIS FRATERNA GVLIELMO GILBERD
SENIORI ARMIGERO & MEDICINÆ.
HIC PRIMÆV. FILIVS HIERONIMI GILBERD
ARMIGERI NAT' ERAT VILLÆ COLCESTRIÆ
STVDVIT CANTABRICIÆ ARTEM MEDICAM
SVMMIS LAVDIBVS PARIQ. FELICITATE PER
TRIGINTA PL. ANNOS LONDINI EXERCVIT
HINC AVLA ACCERSIT IN GYMN V REGINÆ
ELIZABETHÆ FAVOREM ACCEPTVS FVIT
CVI VT SVCCESSORI REGI IACOBO SERVIVIT
ARHIATROS LIBRVM DE MAGNETE APVD
EXTEROS CELEBREM IN REMNAVTICA
COMPOSVIT OBIIT ANNO REDEMPTIONIS
HVMANÆ 1603 NOVEMBRIS VLTIMO
ÆTATIS SVÆ 63

MONUMENT TO DR. GILBERD AT TRINITY CHURCH,
COLCHESTER.

PARLIAMENTARY REPRESENTATIVES OF
COLCHESTER FROM THE RESTORATION.

1660   Sir Harbottle Grimston.
        John Shaw.

1701   Sir Isaac Rebow.
        Sir Thomas Cook.

1741   Charles Gray.
        S. Savill.

1784   Sir E. Affleck, Bart.
        Christopher Potter.

1790   Robert Thornton (W.)
        Lord Muncaster (C.)

1806   Robert Thornton.
        Wm. Tuffnell.

  807   R. H. Davis (C.)
        Robert Thornton (C.)

1812   H. Davis.
        Robert Thornton.

1818   James B. Wildman (C.)
        Daniel Whittle Harvey (R.)

1820   D. W. Harvey.
        J. B. Wildman.

1830   D. W. Harvey.
        A. Spottiswood (C.)

1831   W. Mayhew (W.) vice Spottiswood unseated.

1831   D. W. Harvey.
        W. Mayhew.

1832   Richard Sanderson (C.)
       D. W. Harvey.

1835 ⎫
1837 ⎬ R. Sanderson.
1841 ⎭ Sir G. H. Smyth (C.)

1847   Sir G. H. Smyth (Protectionist.)
       Joseph A. Hardcastle (L.)

1850   Lord J. R. Manners (Protectionist.)
          (on retirement of Sir G. H. Smyth.)

1852   W. W. Hawkins (Protectionist.)
       Lord John Manners.

1857 ⎫ John Gurdon Rebow (L.)
Feb. ⎭ Taverner J. Miller (C.)

1857 ⎫ Taverner J. Miller.
Apr. ⎭ John Gurdon Rebow.

1859   Taverner J. Miller.
       Philip O. Papillon (C.)

1865   John Gurdon Rebow.
       Taverner J. Miller.

1867   E. K. Karslake, Q.C. (C.)
          (on resignation of T. J. Miller.)

1868   J. Gurdon Rebow.
       W. Brewer, M.D. (L.)

1870   Col. A. Learmonth (C.)
          (on death of Mr. Rebow.)

1874   Col. A. Learmonth.
       Herbert B. Praed (C.)

1880   R. K. Causton (L.)
       W. Willis (L.)

1885   After Redistribution of Seats.
       H. J. Trotter (C.)

1888   Lord Brooke (C.)

COMPLETE LIST OF COLCHESTER
MAYORS.

In the following list the eight Mayors marked with an asterisk* are the Mayors who died during their office. Those marked † were for some cause removed before their term of office had expired. G. Wegg, jun. (1740), marked ‡, was elected, but not sworn. A *mandamus* was sent, and on March 9th, 1740, Jeremiah Daniell, senior, was elected, but he died in Feb., 1741.

1635   Daniel Cole.
1636   Robert Buxton.
1637   Henry Barrington.
1638   John Firlie (or Furley.)
1639   John Langley.
1640   Robert Talcott.*
1641   Henry Barrington.
1641   Thos. Wade.
1642   Ralph Harrison.
1643   Thomas Lawrence.
1644   John Cox.
1645   Robert Buxton.
1646   John Langley.
1647   William Cooke.
1648   Henry Barrington.
1649   Thomas Wade.
1650   John Furlie.
1651   Richard Greene.

1652	John Radhams.
1653	Thos. Peeke.
1654	Thos. Reynolds.
1655	Thos. Lawrence.
1656	John Vickers.
1657	Nicholas Beason.
1658	Henry Barrington.†
1659	John Radhams.
1659	Thos. Peeke.
1660	John Gale.
1661	John Milbank.†
1662	Henry Lambe.
1662	Thos. Rennolds.
1663	William Moor.
1664	Thos. Wade.
1665	Thos. Talbot.
1666	Wm. Flannar.
1667	Andrew Fromantcele.
1668	Ralph Creffield.
1669	Henry Lambe.
1670	William Moor.
1671	John Rayner.
1672	Nathaniel Lawrence.
1673	Ralph Creffield.
1674	Henry Lambe.
1675	Alexander Hinmers.
1676	Thos. Greene.
1677	Ralph Creffield.
1678	John Rayner.
1679	Nathaniel Lawrence.
1680	Ralph Creffield.
1681	Wm. Moor.
1682	Thos. Greene.
1683	Nathaniel Lawrence.

1684 John Stilleman.

1685 Wm. Flannar.

1686 Samuel Mott.

1687 Alexander Hindmers.†

1687 John Milbank.

1688 John Milbank.

1689 John Potter.

1690 Benjamin Cock.

1691 John Seabrook.

1692 John Stileman.

1693 Samuel Mott.

1694 Wm. Moore.

1695 John Beason.*

1696 John Seabrook.

1696 Nath. Lawrence, jun.

1697 Ralph Creffield, jun.

1698 Wm. Boys.

1699 Wm. Francis.

1700 John Potter.

1701 Samuel Fetherstone.

1702 Ralph Creffield, jun.

1703 Samuel Angier.

1704 Nath. Lawrence, jun.

1705 John Rainham.

1706 James Lawrence.

1707 George Clark.

1708 John Pepper.*

1709 Nath. Lawrence, sen.

1709 Samuel Angier.

1710 Nath. Lawrence, jun.

1711 James Lawrence.

1712 Peter Johnson.

1713 James Lawrence.

1714 George Clark.

1715 Peter Johnson.

1716 Sir Isaac Rebow, Kt.

1717 Thos. Grigson.

1718 Robt. Clark.

1719 Thos. Grigson.*

1719 Nathaniel Lawrence.

1720 Jeremiah Daniell.

1721 Arthur Winsley.

1722 Edmund Raynham.

1723 Samuel Jarrold.

1724 Peter Johnson.

1725 Jeremiah Daniell.

1726 Matthew Martin.

1727 Sir Ralph Creffield, Kt.

1728 John Blatch.

1729 Jas. Boys (or Boyce).

1730 Joseph Duffield.

1731 John Blatch.

1732 Thos. Carew.

1733 James Boys.

1734 Joseph Duffield.

1735 John Blatch.

1736 Thos. Carew.

1737 James Boys.

1738 Joseph Duffield.

1739 John Blatch.

1740 G. Wegg, jun.‡

1740 Jeremiah Daniell.*

[From the year 1740 to 1763, there being no Charter in existence, no Mayor could be appointed.]

1763 Thos. Clamtree.

1764 Henry Lodge.

1765 Thos. Wilshire.

1766 Thos. Bayles.

1767   Samuel Ennew.

1768   James Robjent.

1769   Jordan Harris Lisle.

1770   John King.

1771   Solomon Smith.*

1772   Thos. Clamtree.

1772   Thos. Bayles.

1773   Thos. Clamtree.

1774   John Baker.*

1775   John King.

1775   Thos. Clamtree.

1776   Thos. Boggis.

1777   Thos. Clamtree.

1778   John King.

1779   Thos. Clamtree.

1780   Thos. Boggis.

1781   John King.

1782   Stephen Betts.

1783   Wm. Seabor.

1784   Samuel Ennew.

1785   Edmund Lilley.

1786   Wm. Argent.

1787   Edward Capstack.

1788   Bezaliel Angier.

1789   Edmund Lilley.

1790   Wm. Swinborne.

1791   John Gibson.

1792   Nathaniel Barlow.

1793   Newton Tills.

1794   Wm. Phillips.

1795   Wm. Bunnell.

1796   Wm. Mason.

1797   Thos. Hedge.

1798   Wm. Phillips.

1799   Robert Hewes.
1800   Wm. Smith.
1801   Thos. Hedge.
1802   Wm. Phillips.
1803   Wm. Bunnell.
1804   Thos. Hedge.
1805   Wm. Sparling.
1806   Wm. Smith.
1807   Thos. Hedge, jun.
1808   Thos. Hedge.
1809   Wm. Smith.
1810   Francis Tillett Abell.
1811   Francis Smythies.
1812   John Bridge.†
1813   Wm. Smith.
1813   Wm. Sparling.
1814   John King.
1815   Edward Clay.
1816   Wm. Argent.
1817   Edward Clay.
1818   Wm. Argent.
1819   Frincis Tillett Abell.
1820   John Clay.
1821   Jas. Boggis.
1822   Wm. Smith.
1823   John Clay.
1824   Samuel Clay.
1825   John Clay.
1826   Edward Clay (St. Leonard's).
1827   John Clay.
1828   Wm. Sparling.
1829   Edward Clay (Greenstead).
1830   Wm. Smith.
1831   Wm. Sparling.

1832   Edward Clay (Greenstead).

1833   Wm. Smith.

1834   Roger Nunn.

[Dr. Nunn held office till 31st Dec., 1835, when the Municipal Reform Act came into operation.]

Mayors subsequent to the passing of the Act for the Regulation of Municipal Corporations in England and Wales (5th and 6th WM. IV., cap. 76). Taken from the Minute Books of the Council :—

1836   Geo. Savill (Jan. 1.)

1836   John Chaplin (Nov. 9.)

1837   Saml. Green Cooke.

1838   Geo. Bawtree.

1839   Saml. Green Cooke.

1840   Thos. J. Turner.

1841   Henry Vint.

1842   Roger Nunn.

1843   Henry Vint.

1844   Henry Wolton.

1845   Henry Wolton.

1846   Wm. Bolton Smith.

1847   Henry Wolton.

1848   Chas. Henry Hawkins.

1849   Edward Williams.

1850   Joseph Cooke.

1851   Arthur Louis Laing.

1852   Francis Smythies.

1853   Henry Wolton.

1854   Edward Williams.

1855   Joseph Cooke.

1856   Henry Wolton.

1857   Peter Martin Duncan.

1858   Arthur Louis Laing.

1859   Edward Williams.
1860   Francis Smythies.
1861   Henry Wolton.
1862   Edward Williams.
1863   John F. Bishop.
1864   John F. Bishop.
1865   Chas. Hy. Hawkins.
1866   P. O. Papillon.
1867   J. F. Bishop.
1868   Francis Smythies.
1869   J. F. Bishop.
1870   C. H. Hawkins.
1871   C. H. Hawkins.
1872   J. F. Bishop.
1873   Edwd. A. Round.
1874   J. F. Bishop.
1875   P. O. Papillon.
1876   J. F. Bishop.
1877   Thomas Moy.
1878   Thomas Moy.
1879   John Kent.
1880   S. Chaplin.
1881   J. B. Harvey.
1882   J. B. Harvey.
1883   Alfred Francis.*
1884   J. B. Harvey.
1884   H. J. Gurdon-Rebow.
1885   Henry Laver.
1886   H. G. Egerton Green.
1887   J. N. Paxman.
1888   E. J. Sanders.
1889   Asher Prior.
1890   L. J. Watts.
1891   Wilson Marriage.

PUBLICATIONS BY

BENHAM & Co.,

24, HIGH STREET, COLCHESTER.

THE TENDRING HUNDRED

IN THE OLDEN TIME,

A Series of Sketches, by the late J. YELLOLY WATSON, F.G.S., J.P., Essex.   Third Edition.   Demy 8vo., Cloth.

Price, 5/-.   Post free, 5/4.

"There was a theory started a few years ago and ventilated, if we remember rightly, by Charles Dickens in *Household Words*, that the earth might be likened to a well balanced saucer or plate, the indented parts, like gravy receptacles, filled with water. Thus, with a slight tilt the water might be made to rush from one side to the other, flooding the dry parts and leaving the old seas dry; and thus, from a great tilt the theorist accounted for the deluge. At any rate there can be no doubt whatever that much of what is now dry land was formerly sea and our seas dry land. Around Harwich and Walton, and far away inland, marine shells and other striking proofs of this in coprolites, &c , are found embedded in the soil, and the sea is fast claiming her own again. The town of Orwell went ages ago, and the stones of the "West Rock," part of its own building materials, have been ground up into cement for London builders. Old Walton has gone, and now, if it were not for "horses," and "groins" and seawalls, and breakwaters, the Tendring Hundred would gradually but surely be devoured by the "sad sea waves." (From *The Tendring Hundred in the Olden Time* pp. 4, 5.)

GUIDE TO COLCHESTER

AND ITS ENVIRONS,

With Notes on the Flora and Entomology of the District. A New, Revised, and Enlarged Edition, with a Map of the Town, and numerous Illustrations. Crown 8vo.

Post free, 1/3.

" The best things in England are not known to the English people. These go abroad to be sentimental over historical antiquities, with which England abounds. In few parts of the kingdom are there more abundant remains of the olden time than in and about Colchester. The town is still a pictorial history of Briton, Roman, Saxon, Norman, and Englishman. Here was the first Roman Colony founded in Britain. Here reigned, that is in legend, the famous King Cole; and legendary lore tells us that his daughter Helena was the mother of Constantine! Colchester Castle is the largest Norman keep in the Country. The Colchester Garrison gave Fairfax more trouble than any other against which he flung himself and his battalions. Finally, here was the Moot Hall, the oldest municipal building in the Kingdom. *Was*, alas! for about thirty years ago it was improved off the face of the earth, and the guilty improvers have been ever since under the *Anathema Maranatha* of all true antiquarians. A trip to Colchester is a thing to be recommended, accepted, and enjoyed. Although we do not endorse every assertion in this Guide, we may safely say that every explorer in, and especially round, this most interesting city, will find great advantage in going by its directions."—*Athenæum.*

AMONG THE TOMBS OF COLCHESTER.

An account of all the Monuments, Tablets, Epitaphs, and
Tombs in the various Church and Grave Yards in the
Town possessing features of archæological, historical, or
other interest.   In Paper Wrapper.

Price, 6d.   Post free, 7d.

VNDER   THIS
MARBLE   LY   THE
BODIES   OF   THE
TWO   MOST   VALI
ANT   CAPTAINS
S ʀ   CHARLES
LVCAS   AND   S ʀ
GEORGE   LISLE
KNIGHTS   WHO
FOR   THEIR   EMI
NENT   LOYALTY
TO   THEIR   SOVE
RAIN   WERE   ON
THE 28th DAY OF AV
GVST 1648 BY THE
COMMAND   OF   S ʀ
THOMAS   FAIR
FAX   THEN   GENE
RAL   OF   THE   PAR
LIAMENT   ARMY   IN
COLD   BLOOD   BARBA
ROVSLY   MVRDERED.

(From *Among the Tombs of Colchester*, page 12.)

"The anonymous compiler of this little pamphlet has performed
for Colchester a task which should be undertaken in every important
town in England.   Quaint and curious epitaphs, as well as those of
historical and biographical interest, have from the first been
chronicled in the columns of "N. & Q."   The burial-grounds of
Colchester abound in tombstones which have a value both for the
general and local antiquary, and by the aid of this tiny work they
will be preserved for many generations to come.   In Essex, as in
other parts of the country, the duty of preserving many important
epitaphs has been neglected until the feet of the passers-by have
made them illegible."—*Notes and Queries*.

K

THE HISTORY AND ANTIQUITIES OF COLCHESTER CASTLE,

Together with an Introductory Chapter on Ancient Colchester. Demy 8vo., 147 pp., with an illustration and ground-plans.

Cloth, 3/-.   Boards, 2/6.   Postage, 3d.

This work, which is the result of considerable research, contains fresh and exhaustive information on the origin, history, associations, and architecture of the Castle, together with a full account of its little-known demesnes. It also comprises many fresh facts on the siege of Colchester and the general history of the Town.

OPINIONS OF THE PRESS.

"As a critical and exhaustive monograph on this 'vastest of Norman donjons' it is a valuable contribution not only to the local, but to the general, history of England."—*Academy*.

"Probably the most important contribution to the history of Colchester since the days of the indefatigable Morant . . . . There can be no question that the *History and Antiquities of Colchester* will be the standard work of reference on the subject with which it deals."—*Essex Standard*.

"A nicely bound and well printed little volume."—*Chelmsford Chronicle*.

TALES OF THE NORTH SEA,
By C. E. B.

Price, 4d.   Post free, 5d.

"The tales are nine in number, and they are such stories as we might fairly expect to hear from the great sea if it could but talk, instead of only moaning and roaring. Each tale is briefly but carefully and pleasantly told, and they are interspersed here and there with some really good verses."—*Essex Standard*.

"Here is a story-teller of a very remarkable character, like none we have perused for many a day, as he goes right off the beaten track, if beaten track is a right expression for the sea, which is chiefly his theme . . . . . . Yet, withal, we cannot divest ourselves of the sensation that there is some thing uncanny in these narratives; they are so strange in matter, and oddly stated."—*Court Journal*.

"Many just thoughts and a good deal of information about the sea in a very enticing form."—*Western Morning News*.

"We were much struck with their power and pathos. They are at once intensely interesting and touching, and anybody who begins to read them, will certainly read on to the end."—*Essex County Chronicle*.

GUIDE TO WALTON, CLACTON & FRINTON,

With numerous Illustrations.

Price, 4d.   Post free, 5d.

HISTORY OF COLCHESTER.

By HENRY LAVER, Esq., F.L.S., Illustrated.

Price, 2d.   Post free, 2½d.

THE ESSEX LABOURER DRAWN FROM LIFE

With 29 Illustrations.

Price, 6d.   Post free 6½d.

NOTES ON THE HISTORY OF MALDON,

By E. A. FITCH, Esq.

Price, 3d.   Post free, 3½d.

BENHAM & Co.,

PRINTERS & PUBLISHERS,

24, HIGH STREET,

COLCHESTER.

THE following Books relating to Essex are frequently in stock, or can in most cases, be procured to order. As there are several editions of some works, the dates given must be considered approximate. Particulars as to price, &c., may be obtained from

T. FORSTER,

Ye Olde Booke Shoppe,

101, *High Street,*

 ### COLCHESTER.

AGRICULTURE of the County of Essex, by the
Secretary of the Board of Agriculture, illustrated, 2 vols., 8vo.
1807.

ANNALS OF EVANGELICAL NONCONFORMITY in
the County of Essex, from the time of Wycliffe to the
Restoration; with memorials of the Essex Ministers who
were ejected or silenced in 1660-62, by T. W. Davids, of the
Congregational Chapel, Lion Walk, Colchester.   1863.

ANCIENT MANORIAL CUSTOMS, TENURES, &c.,
of the County of Essex, by Charnock.

AUDLEY END. (History of), by Lord Braybrooke, 4to.
1836.

AUTOBIOGRAPHY OF AN ENGLISH GAME-
KEEPER—John Wilkins, of Stanstead. Edited by Byng &
Stephens, 8vo, illustrated.   (In the press.)

BIRDS OF ESSEX. A contribution to the Natural
History of the County, by Miller Christy, 8vo, illustrated.
1890.

Vol. II. of the Essex Field Club—Special Memoirs.

BIRD NESTING AND BIRD SKINNING, by
E. Newman; revised and rewritten by Miller Christy, 1/-.
1888.

BYGONE ESSEX. Chapters in the Ancient History
and Antiquities of the County, by various contributors.
(In the press.)

Will be issued early in 1892 at 5/- to Subscribers—on day of
publication the price will be raised to 7/6.

Subscribers' names received by the Publisher—T. Forster,
Colchester.

BRAINTREE UNION. Proceedings in reference to the
Appointment of a Chaplain, by an Elected Guardian, 8vo.,
29 pp.   Braintree, 1838.

BRAINTREE CHURCH RATE CASE. Report of the
Judgments, Gosling v. Veley, in 1850, 8vo, 44 pp.   1850.

BRENTWOOD FREE GRAMMAR SCHOOL. An
Enquiry into its Revenues and Abuses, 8vo, 104 pp.   1823.

BURGESS, REV. W. Vicar of Thorpe, Kirby, and
Walton. Sermons—Doctrinal and Practical 8vo.   1863.

COLCHESTER CASTLE, its History and Antiquities,
by H. Round.   1882.

COLCHESTER CASTLE, a Roman Building, a few
remarks on the above book, by G. Buckler, 8vo, 16 pp.,
not published.   1882.

COLCHESTER CASTLE, built by a Colony of Romans, as a Temple to their deified Emperor, Claudius Cæsar, by H. Jenkins, Rector of Stanway, 8vo, with eight illustrations, 1853.

COLCHESTER CASTLE, not a Roman Temple, being a review of the above Lecture, by E. L. Cutts, 8vo, illustrated. 1853.

An appendix to the above Lecture, together with a reply to the animadversions of the Rev. E. L. Cutts, 8vo. 1853.

COLCHESTER CASTLE, shown to have once been the Templed Citadel, which the Romans raised to their Emperor Claudius, at Colonia Camulodunum, by H. Jenkins, 8vo. 1861. Revised edition. 1869.

COLCHESTER CASTLE, a Roman Building, and the oldest and noblest Monument of the Romans in Britain, by G. Buckler, author of "Twenty-two of the Churches of Essex." 8vo, illustrated. 1876.

COLCHESTER CASTLE, its founders, governors and owners, with description of St. Botolph's Priory, by B. Golding, 6d. 1892.

COLCHESTER. (An account of the ancient Borough, Town of) from the earliest period to the present time, by R. Swinborne, sm. 8vo, with seven engravings. N.D.

COLCHESTER. (Sketches of Ancient), by J. Y. Watson, 8vo. 1879.

COLCHESTER. (Guide to) and its environs, with notes on the Flora and Entomology of the District, 1/-.

COLCHESTER, its History and Antiquities. Selected from the most approved Authors, by M. Carter.

Of this work there are several editions, the first being scarce, the others fairly common.

COLCHESTER. (History and description of the Ancient Town and Borough of,) by Thomas Cromwell, 8vo, illustrated. Of this work there are several editions.

COLCHESTER. (Siege of,) or an event of the Civil War, A.D., 1648, by G. F. Townsend, 8vo, illustrated. N.D.

COLCHESTER. Historical Sketch of the Parish of St. Martin. 6d. 1891.

COLCHESTER. (The History and description of,) the Camulodunum of the Britons, and the first Roman Colony of Britain, with an account of the Antiquities of that most ancient Borough (by Strutt,) 8vo, usually in two volumes. 1803.

COLCHESTER. Short History of the Town, by Dr. H. Laver, illustrated, 3d., post free

COLCHESTER. (Morant's History, see Essex.)

COLCHESTER. (Charities of,) Report of Official Enquiry held in Colchester, in 1886, before W. Good, 1/-. Colchester, 1886.

COLCHESTER. (History of,) by E. L. Cutts, contains a Chapter on the Jewish Quarter of the Town, 3/6. 1888.

COLCHESTER. Story of the Siege, by A. Penn, sewed, 6d. Colchester, 1888.

COLCHESTER. (Report of St. Alban's Diocesan Conference at,) in 1889, 6d. Colchester, 1889.

COLCHESTER MUSEUM. Catalogue of the Antiquities therein, illustrated, 8vo.

COLCHESTER'S TEARES, affecting and afflicting City and Country, by several persons of quality, 1648, and several later reprints, 8vo and 4to.

COLCHESTER OYSTER FEAST. A Souvenir of the one given on October 22, 1891, by L. J. Watts, Mayor, 8vo, illustrated, 1/-. 1891.

CHARTER (The New,) granted to the Mayor and Commonalty of Colchester in 1763, with recitals of the Old Charters confirmed by the present, 8vo. 1764.

CHARTERS granted to the Borough of Harwich by James I. and Charles II., translated from the original Latin by order of the Corporation, 4to. 1798.

CHELMSFORD. (Narrative of the late deplorable fire at), on March 19, 1808, with ground plan of the part of the Town destroyed, by Rt Kelham, a witness of the Fire, 8vo. 1808.

A general and circumstantial account of the above fire, by W. W. Wall, a spectator, 8vo. 1804.

COPENHAGEN, its Siege and Capture by the British in 1807, with frontispiece, 42 pp. Colchester, N.D.

CHRISTIAN RELIGION'S Appeal from the groundless prejudices of the Sceptic to the Bar of Common Reason, by J. Smith, Rector of St. Mary's, Colchester, small folio. 1675.

COGGESHALL. Its History, with an Account of the Church, Abbey, Manors, &c., by G. F. Beaumont, illustrated, 8vo, cloth, 7/6. Coggeshall, 1890.

COGGESHALL. Radulphi Abbatis Coggeshal, opera quæ supersunt curante Alf. John Donkin, nunc Primum edita, 8vo. boards, uncut, only 25 copies printed, scarce, with portrait of Dunkin. Noviomago, 1856

COGGESHALL (History of,) with an account of its Church, Abbey, Manors, &c., by G. F. Beaumont. 8vo., illustrated. Coggeshall, 1890.

COGGESHALL (The Annals of,) by Bryan Dale, sm. 8vo., illustrated. Coggeshall, 1863.

COPFORD, ESSEX, A Short Account of the Church, Mural Paintings, etc., by B. Ruck-Keene, with View of Church, 1/- Coggeshall, 1890.

DOMESDAY BOOK, relating to Essex, translated by T. C. Chisenhale Marsh, 4to.

DORLING'S GUIDE to Walton, Clacton and the neighbouring Towns, to which is added a guide from Walton to London by Steam Boat, cloth, illustrated.

DAGENHAM BEACH, by Perry, 8vo. 1721.

Ditto, by Boswell, 12mo. 1717.

EAST ANGLIAN EARTHQUAKE, on April 22, 1884. Full Report on it, by Raphael Meldola & W. White, 8vo, with maps and illustrations.

Vol. 1 of the Essex Field Club, Special Memoirs. 1885.

EARTHQUAKE IN EAST-ESSEX, on April 22, 1884. Reprinted from the Essex Telegraph, 1/-

ESSEX FIELD CLUB. The organ of this Club, "The Essex Naturalist," is issued monthly, price to Members, 4/6, to Non-Members, 9/- per annum. Previous to its commencement. they issued Transactions and Proceedings, the early volumes being very scarce.

THE REPRINTED PAPERS INCLUDE—

Elephant Hunting in Essex, by Walker.
Report on Explorations at Ambresbury Banks
Report on Explorations at Loughton Camp.
Report on the Exploration of the Essex Dencholes.
Lichen Flora of Epping Forest, by Crombie.
Memoir of the late G. S. Gibson.
Papers on the protection of Wild Animals and Plants, and on the condition of Epping Forest, &c.
For special Memoirs, see—
East Anglian Earthquake.
Birds of Essex.

ESSEX. (The Ancient Sepulchral Monuments of,) by
G. F. Chancellor, 4to, illustrated, £4 4s. *nett.*

ESSEX. (The people's History of,) from the earliest
ages to the present time, with account of the Hundreds and
Boroughs, and descriptive sketches of their antiquities and
ruins, &c., by D. W. Coller, 8vo, Chelmsford.   1861.

ESSEX REVIEW. A quarterly Journal devoted to
the study of the antiquities, &c. of the County, 5/- per annum
if paid in advance, 1/6 per part.   1892.

ESSEX. An Historical and Chorographical description
of the county, by John Norden, 1594, reprinted by the Camden
Society.   1840.

ESSEX. (Durrant's handbook for,) or *guide* to the
principal objects of interest in each Parish, with an introduction
treating of the History, Geology, Antiquities, &c. of the
County, by Miller Christy, 8vo, 237 pp., 2/6.   1887.

EASTERN ENGLAND. (Royal Illustrated History of,)
Civil, Military, Political, and Ecclesiastical, from the earliest
period to the present time, by A. D. Bayne, 2 vols, thick 8vo,
Great Yarmouth, N.D.

ESSEX. The History and Antiquities of the County,
by P. Morant, Rector of St. Mary-at-the-Walls, Colchester
2 vols, folio.   1768'.

   This work was reprinted (in numbers) in 1817, at Chelmsford,
but without plates or date.

   Morant also issued the History of Colchester separately.
There are two editions.

ESSEX DIALECT. (A glossary of the,) by Charnock,
8vo.   1880.

ESSEX. The History and Topography of the County,
by Thomas Wright, illustrated by a series of views taken on
the spot, by Arnold, Bartlett and others, 4to, mostly in two
volumes.   1836.

ESSEX. (The Farming of), a report, by R. Baker of
Writtle, 6d.   1844.

EASTERN ENGLAND, from the Thames to the
Humber, by W. White, with map, 2 vols.   1865.

ECCLESIASTICAL ARCHITECTURE of the County,
from the Norman Era to the sixteenth Century, by Hadfield,
77 full-page plates, folio.   London, N.D.

ESSEX COUNTY ELECTION. Speeches delivered at the Hustings, and the Proceedings during Fifteen Days' Contest between Western, Tyrell, and Wellesley, in 1830, with an impartial Selection of the Squibs and Handbills.

Chelmsford, 1830.

ESSEX HARMONY, being a choice collection of Songs, Catches, Canons, Epigrams, &c., for two to nine voices from the works of the most Eminent Masters. N.D.

ESSEX NOTE BOOK and Suffolk Gleaner, "A snapper up of unconsidered Trifles," containing upwards of 400 Notes of Local Interest on Matters relating to County, illustrated, sm. 4to, cloth, very scarce, 15/-. 1884-5.

ESSEX (Excursions in the County of). Historical and Topographical Delineations of every Town and Village, with Descriptions of the Residences of the Nobility and Gentry, 100 engravings. 1818.

ESSEX (History of) from Cox's Britanniæ, with map of County, 103 pp.

ESSEX LITERARY JOURNAL, or Monthly Repository of Literature, and the Arts and Sciences connected with the County, issued in 12 parts, 4to. Chelmsford, 1839.

ESSEX. A new and complete History of Essex, from a late survey, by a gentleman, published under the patronage and direction of Peter Muilman, 6 vols., illustrated.

Chelmsford, 1769-72.

The fifteen following items are reprints by Charles Clarke, of Totham ; some of them passed through several editions, mostly from his Private Press.

A DOCTOR'S "DO"-INGS ; or the entrapped Heiress of Witham. A satirical poem, by Charles Clarke.

ENGLISH COOKERY, Five Hundred Years ago, exhibited in sixty "Nyms," or Receipts, from a manuscript compiled about 1390, by the Master Cooks of Richard II. Black Letter, with a running glossary and notes. 1849.

FALSE PROPHETS DISCOVERED, being a true story of the lives and deaths of two Weavers, of Colchester ; they affirmed that they were the Prophets mentioned in Revelation XI., Reprinted from the edition of 1642, with an Appendix, containing an account of the Inworth Prophetess of 1797. 1844.

FAIRLOP AND ITS FOUNDER ; or Facts and Fun for the Forest Frolickers, by a Famed First Friday Fairgoer, with the curious Will of Mr. Day, of Wapping, and five Poems on Fairlop. 1847.

HUMAN FATE: a Poem, by Sir Egerton Brydges. Reprint by C. Clarke.

JOHN NOAKES AND MARY STYLES; or "an Essex Calf's" visit to Tiptree Races; a Poem, exhibiting some of the most striking lingual localisms peculiar to Essex, with a Glossary. 1839.

METRICAL MIRTH about Marriageable Misses; or the Modern Mode in Matters Matrimonial, by a Lover of Honest Mothers and Gentle Daughters. 1848.

MIRTH AND METRE; or Rhymes, "Raps," and Rhapsodies, by C. C.

NARRATIVE OF THE MIRACULOUS CURE OF ANNE MUNNINGS, of Colchester, by Faith, Prayer, and Anointing with Oil, in 1705.

PLEASANT QUIPPES FOR UPSTART NEWFAN- GLED GENTLEWOMEN, by Stephen Gosson. Reprint by C. C.

POOR ROBIN'S TRUE CHARACTER OF A SCOLD; or, the Shrew's Looking-glass, dedicated to all Domineering Dames, Wives Rampant, Cuckolds Couchant, and Hen-peckt Sneaks, in City or Country (reprinted from the Edition of 1678), Black Letter. 1848.

PULPIT ORATORY, four Centuries ago. Two sermons preached in 1432.

SCARCITY AND EXCELLENCY OF VIRTUOUS WOMEN, by J. Colby, of Maldon. Reprint by C. C.

TIPTREE FAIR IN 1844. A curious specimen of the "Unlettered Muse," with notes. 1848.

TIPTREE RACES; a Poem (with notes), to which is added an Historical Account of Tiptree Heath, Priory, and Fair; also a Poem inscribed to Thomas Hood, Esq., of Lake House, Wemstead, each line ends with 4 rhymes.

FOOTSTEPS OF St. PAUL IN ROME, by S. Russell Forbes, a native of Colchester. It gives a Genealogical table tracing the descent of Helena and Constantine, from the British King Caractacus, 8vo, illustrated. 2/-

FELSTEAD CHARITIES. Scheme for the management and administration of the Estates and Revenues, approved of by the Court of Chancery in 1851, 8vo. 1852.

FELSTEAD SCHOOL (A History of), with some account of the Founder and his Descendants, by John Sargeaunt, 8vo, illustrated, 4/- nett. Chelmsford, 1889.

FELIX HALL (Descriptive Sketch of the collection of works of Ancient Greek and Roman Art at); a paper read at the Meeting of the Essex Archæological Society in 1863, by the Rev. J. H. Marsden, 4to, illustrated, scarce.

GIBSON'S FLORA OF ESSEX, or a list of the Flowering Plants and Ferns found in the County, 8vo.   1862.

GUIDES. These are too numerous to mention; they are issued for almost every place in the County, and in many cases there are several editions.

GIBBS, JOHN, formerly Curator of Chelmsford Museum.
First Catechism of Botany, 1/-.
Symmetry of Flowers, 6d.

HALSTEAD, Old and New, by W. J. Evans, 8vo, illustrated.   1886.

HARWICH. An Historical and Archæological Sketch of the Town, by R. Cutler.   Harwich, N.D.

HARWICH (a Season at), with Excursions by Land and Water, to which is added Researches, Historical, Natural and Miscellaneous, by Lindsey, 8vo., illustrated.   Harwich, 1851.

HISTORY OF ESSEX from the earliest period to the present time, with biographical notices of the most distinguished natives, by Ogborne, illustrated, 4to.   1814.

HISTORICAL RECORD of the Forty-fourth, or the East-Essex Regiment, by Carter, illustrated.   Chatham, 1887.

HARWICH AND DOVERCOURT (History of), by Dale, 4to.   1732.

HEDINGHAM CASTLE, its History; by Majendie, folio, illustrated.   1796.

HICKERINGILL (Rev. E.), Rector of All Saints Church, Colchester.
A voluminous writer, mostly in connection with legal cases in which he was connected. He also wrote a history of Jamaica.

INOCULATION (Sermon in defence of), preached at Ingatestone, in 1766, by R. Houlton, 76 pp., scarce.
        Chelmsford, N.D.

JESUS CHRIST (Life of), the Holy Apostles, Evangelists, St. John Baptist, the Blessed Virgin and others, during the first three Centuries, by P. Wright, Vicar of Oakley, illustrated, folio.   N.D.

LAWFORD HALL (The Hall of). Records of an Essex House, and of its proprietors from the Saxon Times to the Reign of Henry VIII, Illustrated, by F. M. Nichols, 42/- nett. 1891.

Of this work only 128 copies were printed mostly for presentation.

MAPLESTEAD. History and Antiquities of the Round Church, with an Historical sketch of the Crusades, by Wallen, illustrated, 8vo. 1836.

MEMORIALS OF THE ANTIQUITIES AND ARCHITECTURE, Family History and Heraldry of the County, by Suckling, 34 full page plates, folio. 1845.

MEMOIR OF CARTER, the Lip Artist of Coggeshall, by Dampier, illustrated. 1850.

MARSH, (Dr. W.,) sometime Rector of St. Peter's, Colchester, his Life by his daughter, with portrait, 8vo. 1867.

NEWCOURT'S REPERTORIUM. An Ecclesiastical Parochial History of the Diocese of London, (this Diocese then included Middlesex and Essex, with parts of Herts and Bucks), with portrait, 2 vols., small folio. 1708.

NUMISMATOLOGY. A monthly magazine, devoted to the study of Coins, edited by T. Forster, Colchester. 1892.

PAPERS in relation to the Ancient Topography of the Eastern Counties of Great Britain, and on the right means of Interpreting the Roman Itinerary, by Taylor, 4to. 1892.

PAGLESHAM OYSTER. Music, Charades, Riddles, &c., by Harris, Hatch and Wiseman, 4to. Rochford, 1870.

PLAIN THOUGHTS on Prophecy, by W. Marsh, Vicar of St. Peter's, Colchester, 8vo. Colchester, N.D.

PARAPHRASE ON THE LORD'S PRAYER, Miscellaneous Poems and Fables in Verse, by Mrs. Winter, of Manningtree, 8vo. 1852.

POLL BOOKS, for the different divisions of the County, for Colchester, Chelmsford, Maldon, &c.

PLESHEY. Some account of its Lords and its Antiquities. 1885:

PLESHEY. Its History and Antiquities, by Gough, 4to. 1803.

PROTOPLAST. A series of papers on the beginnings or First mention of things, the subjects treated of being Matter, Day, Law, Sleep, Sin, Death, Baptism, Promise, &c., by Mrs. Baillie, of Wivenhoe. There are several editions.

ROCHFORD HUNDRED (The History of,) by Philip Benton ; has been coming out in parts for some years.

ROYAL ARCHÆOLOGICAL INSTITUTE OF GREAT BRITAIN AND IRELAND. Full Report of the proceedings at the Colchester Meeting, in August, 1876.

ROMFORD (Memoirs of Old) and other places within the Royal Liberty of Havering-Atte-Bower, by George Terry.
Romford, 1880.

STIFFORD, and more about Stifford, by Palin. 1871-2.

SILKWORM (The Japanese,) Bombyx Yama-maï. Report on its culture in England in 1867-8, by A. Wallace, M.D., of Colchester, 8vo, 1/-. Colchester, 1869.

SPORTSMAN'S DIRECTORY ; or, Park and Game-keeper's Companion, with a description of all kinds of Poaching, &c., by John Mayer, Gamekeeper, 12mo.
Colchester, 1815.

STOCK-HARVARD, its Registers, by Gibson. 1881.

TRUE RELATION of that Honourable, though unfortunate Expedition of Kent, Essex, and Colchester, in 1648, by M. Carter, Quarter-Master General in the King's Forces, and one of the Prisoners who surrendered. There are several editions.

TENDRING HUNDRED IN THE OLDEN TIME. A series of Sketches by J. Yelloly Watson, of Thorpe-le-Soken.
N.D.

TRADE SIGNS OF ESSEX. A popular account of the origin and meanings of the Public House and other signs, now or formerly found in the County, by Miller Christy, 8vo, illustrated. 1887.

TOPOGRAPHICAL and Statistical Descriptions of every County in England and Scotland, with separate map of each county, also description of each County in Wales, with 2 maps, one of the northern and the other the southern counties, by G. A. Cooke, 19 vols. V.Y.

TWENTY-TWO OF THE CHURCHES OF ESSEX, Architecturally described and illustrated, by Buckler, 8vo. 1856.

UPMINSTER (Sketches of), by Wilson, sm. 4to. 1856.

WALTHAMSTOW. Its Past, Present, and Future History, with Notes on the Objects of Interest in the surrounding Neighbourhood, 8vo. Tweedie, Walthamstow, 1861.

WALTHAM ABBEY. History of the Town and Abbey from the Foundation to the present time by J. Farmer, to which is added the History of Abbeys from 977 to the Reign of Queen Elizabeth. 1735.

WALTHAM HOLY CROSS ABBEY, by Buckler, 4to, illustrated.

WALTHAM ABBEY (History of,) by Fuller. 1840.